MERCHANT OF DEATH

AN ALEX MASON THRILLER

DAVID ARCHER

BLAKE BANNER

RIGHTHOUSE

PRAISE FOR ALEX MASON

"It is brutal, wastes no time, and is full of action."

"Better than Bond, Bourne, or Reacher."

"For fans of Clancy, Mitch App, and Brad Taylor."

"Same level as Patterson or Baldacci."

"This book is filled with action, intrigue, espionage, and everything else lovers of a good thriller want."

ISBN-13: 978-1-63696-419-5

ISBN-10: 1-63696-419-2

Cover design by: Damonza

Printed in the United States of America

www.righthouse.com

www.instagram.com/righthousebooks

www.facebook.com/righthousebooks

twitter.com/righthousebooks

ALEX MASON THRILLERS
Odin (Book 1)
Ice Cold Spy (Book 2)
Mason's Law (Book 3)
Assets and Liabilities (Book 4)
Russian Roulette (Book 5)
Executive Order (Book 6)
Dead Man Talking (Book 7)
All The King's Men (Book 8)
Flashpoint (Book 9)
Brotherhood of the Goat (Book 10)
Dead Hot (Book 11)
Blood on Megiddo (Book 12)
Son of Hell (Book 13)
Merchant of Death (Book 14)

PROLOGUE

PETER BLAKELOCK WAS ON THE ISLAND OF MENORCA, in the Mediterranean, looking for Yasha Orlev. Because he had absconded from DC with a flash drive containing information that, potentially, could rock the world. The drive contained a report commissioned by the man known as Nero, head of the shadowy ODIN organization which both ran and coordinated the Five Eyes intelligence gathering network.

And also, officially at least, didn't really exist.

Precisely what was on the drive only three people had known: Nero, Professor David Geller, who had produced the content, and Orlev, his closest friend and colleague. They had known what was on it and now, with Geller shot dead in his apartment in London, they also knew there were those who thought it was worth killing for.

Put more precisely, Nero and Orlev were now in no doubt that the drive had the potential to cripple the United States and bring the Earth to the brink of World War III. At a mere one and a half inches in length, the drive had suddenly become the most valuable and dangerous item on the planet—and it had vanished, along with Yasha Orlev.

Blakelock had met Yasha Orlev at the Forbidden Fruit Club on L Street in DC. Orlev had been drunk and looked sullen the way drunk men do when they wake up from their life's dream to discover that their reality has become a nightmare. He was drinking vodka neat and shouting a lot at those who would listen, who were few, and those who wouldn't, who were many. One of those who was listening was Blakelock. He was paying attention because he had been told to by Nero. As Blakelock approached Orlev through the heaving crowd and the spiraling lasers, he recalled Nero's words.

"Orlev is a genius. When genii go off the rails, they fall further than common men. In his case, he is a dangerous genius. Catch him before he falls. He could cause untold damage."

"Hey, Yasha Orlev, isn't it? Peter Blakelock. What are you shouting about, man?"

"Everything," he said and spun his finger, indicating the club, the world, and perhaps the universe, "is a lie. It is all lies. They are lying to us!"

"Yeah? Who are?"

That had made him laugh a lot, and he had poked Blakelock on the chest and shouted above the music.

"The Anunnaki. They are not returning. They are already here! Buy real estate, my friend. Buy real estate in the mountains, high up. Are you a prepper? You should be a prepper. I am an Israeli. Did you know that? We Israelis are preppers by nature. It's in our cultural DNA. They are going to kill everybody."

"You still didn't tell me who 'they' are, Yasha."

He laughed again. "Here is something funny! Who is *going* to kill you is *the most important thing in the world!* Yeah? But who *killed* you—past tense—is the *least* important thing in the world. Crazy, huh?"

He swayed and downed another shot of vodka. Then he tried to focus on Blakelock's face. "It doesn't matter," he said. "It's too late."

"How are you getting home, Yasha?"

"Home? Home is a concept that belongs to the 19th and 20th century. There is no home anymore. Unless there is home in death."

The music throbbed in the darkness, and the lasers fanned out red and blue. Blakelock leaned close and shouted in Orlev's ear.

"Come on, man! This place would drive anyone to depression. You want to get some food and I'll drive you home?"

"You're not gay, are you? I am not gay. I like women."

Blakelock laughed. "I'm not gay, Yasha. We met at the hotel, remember? I'm worried about you, man. You are well over the limit. How are you getting home?"

Orlev had held up one finger. "Home," he said, "is in a cove in Menorca, among the shade of pine trees, with my love on the sand."

"Menorca? You're kidding! I love Menorca. I used to vacation there all the time."

Orlev had laughed again. "Fascinating. I'm gonna piss. Don't move. I'll be back, Like Schwarzenegger." And he had staggered away through the crowd.

That had been the last Peter Blakelock had seen of Yasha Orlev.

Yasha Orlev might have been a genius, but he was no

spook. A little scrounging on international databases which were readily accessible to ODIN showed that he owned a villa on the south coast of the island of Menorca at a secluded bay called Cala Escorxada. The house, from what Blakelock could make out from the satellite pictures, was large and sprawling, with a nice pool, surrounded on four sides by dense pinewoods and just a quarter of a mile from a small bay with cliffs on either side and a sandy beach in between. Presumably where Orlev liked to observe his love sunbathing.

ODIN had booked Blakelock a flight to the *Aeroport de Menorca*, rented him a convertible Mercedes CLE 450 Cabrio, booked him in at the curiously named Experimental Hotel, and told him to bring Yasha Orlev back with him, alive, along with the flash drive plus all computers, laptops, tablets, phones, drives, notes, and anything else that might be related.

All of which led to Peter Blakelock's pulling up after a very roundabout, dusty drive from Mahon outside a large, arched iron gate set in a tall, redbrick wall in the middle of a very dense, shady pine forest. The air was rich with the warm smells of resin, rosemary, and thyme in the copper afternoon as the sun declined toward the western sea.

He climbed out of the car into the dappled shade and tried the gate. It was held closed by a chain wound several times around the central iron bars and secured by a large padlock. He looked north along the road through the tunnel of trees and then south toward the cove, the cliffs, and the beach. There was not a soul to be seen. So he pulled his Glock from under his arm and blew off the lock. Then he carefully unwound the chain and pushed the gates open.

The broad drive led among pine trees to an esplanade. Beyond it was a large balustraded terrace with terracotta tiles surrounding a large, turquoise pool. There were deckchairs and a white wrought iron table and chairs but no people. He stood a while, watching and listening. There was nothing.

He got back in the Mercedes, parked on the esplanade, and then returned to close the gates.

It was a two-story villa with an orange tiled roof which had turned pink against the green trees in the dying sun. It was that time in the early evening when the heat is easing in the air, the sky is turning a deeper blue, and if you're in the right kind of neighborhood, you start to smell barbequed meat and hear the tinkle of ice in tall glasses. Only there was no barbeque on Orlev's terrace, and there were no tinkling glasses. In fact, the only sound was the desultory flutter of wings in the trees and the gentle lapping of the water in his pool.

Blakelock rang the bell and hammered on the front door. There was no reply. So having checked a second time that there was nobody around, he blew out the lock and stepped into the living room. It was bright, with large, distorted oblongs of light lying across the terracotta tiles and sheepskin rugs. The absolute silence was a strange contrast to the bright, comfortable room, the big calico sofa and chairs, the large, bright, impressionist paintings on the walls, and the colored glass vases that stood on shelves and lamp tables here and there, reflecting the light from outside.

The room was broad, with an open fireplace, a dining area, and a short passage that led to a large, stone-flagged kitchen. There, beside the sink, Blakelock found a breakfast plate with toasted breadcrumbs, a demitasse with dried black coffee in it, and a couple of knives with butter on them. One for the butter, one for the toast. A meticulous man.

Back in the living room, there was a heavy pine staircase

that rose to a second floor. With an uncomfortable prickling in the back of his neck, Blakelock climbed the steps.

It was darker upstairs. There was a broad landing and a balustrade. He could make out four doors ahead of him, to right and left. All but one were closed, but he could see that the open one was the one he wanted.

It led into a room that was slipping into dusk. There were sliding glass doors that stood open onto a terracotta terrace. Beyond the terrace was the canopy of the pine woods, and beyond that the dark blue sweep of the Mediterranean. There, a fat, orange moon hung low over the sea.

Yasha Orlev was sitting there with his back to the glass doors. He was at a small table looking out over the forest, toward the moon. Blakelock crossed the room on silent feet and stood in the doorway, watching Orlev. His thin, sandy hair was moving in the evening breeze.

Blakelock took a Camel from his pocket and poked it in his mouth. He didn't light it because he didn't want to leave forensic evidence of his presence at the scene of a murder. He stepped out onto the balcony and hunkered down in front of the dead remains of Yasha Orlev. He was staring with dead eyes at a moon he could not see and would never see again. His hands were resting on the arms of the chair, bound tightly with nylon cord. The only blood was from the toothpicks which had been forced under his fingernails. Cause of death had been the kitchen knife that still protruded from his chest.

Blakelock stepped back into the house through the sliding glass doors. The room was some kind of study or office. There was a computer on a desk to the left, a laptop on a low bookcase against the far wall, and to Blakelock's right, there were three filing cabinets, a long sofa, and a lamp on a small, marble-topped table.

He was aware his priorities had changed. With Yasha Orlev dead, his focus now had to be to recover, as Nero had put it, "... the flash drive, all computers, laptops, tablets, phones, drives, notes, and anything else that might hold information about his and Geller's research and conclusions."

Blakelock disconnected the hard drive from the computer and stacked it with the laptop. He then conducted a thorough and detailed search of the office and found exactly nothing. Which made him pretty certain that was what they were going to find on the computers when he got them back to the lab. Whoever had killed Orlev had cleaned up and taken all his work with him. Nero would not be happy, but more than that, the consequences for the United States and her allies could be catastrophic.

It was a forlorn hope, but Blakelock moved to the first bedroom to continue his search there. The windows were closed, and the room was dark. He put his cell on flashlight, opened the built-in wardrobe, and hunkered down to check the drawers and the panels at the back. There was an empty sports bag, three pairs of shoes, and an iPhone charger that had fallen out of the bag. He set them on the floor and leaned forward to tap the back wall.

That was when the bootlace went around his neck, tightening with terrifying force, cutting off his air. The cell dropped from his hand, casting crazy vertical shadows looming out of the wardrobe, like black messengers of death. He could feel his lungs screaming, his face swelling, his eyes and tongue puffing up. The strength in his attacker's arms was horrific, but Blakelock knew that if he focused on his neck or his lungs, he would die. When you're being strangled you have to think about the other guy's hands. And that's what he did. He reached in his pocket and pulled out his cheap, blue disposable lighter. He was losing the sight in his eyes, his lungs were hurting, and he could feel his consciousness slipping, but the action was automatic. His thumb spun the wheel, the flint sparked, and the gas caught, and then the guy's wrist was burning. Blakelock caught the stench of scorching flesh just before he heard the scream, and suddenly air was rasping through his throat, filling his lungs.

He fell and rolled away, clutching at his neck, wheezing and retching for breath. Over the noise of his own gasping, Blakelock could hear his attacker's feet staggering away, across the room. The guy was still swearing, cursing, and screaming in pain. Still struggling for breath, Blakelock reached for his cell and aimed its beam at the gigantic shadow framed in the door. It turned and charged. He dropped the cell and reached for the Glock under his arm. The brute was fast and strong, and the kick came like an express train and smashed into his arm, sending him sprawling and the Glock spinning across the floor.

The brute hesitated for just a second, unsure whether to go after Blakelock or the gun. Even in his dazed state, with shafts of pain driving through his arm and his chest, that second was all the time he needed. He scrambled, ran three steps, and dove through the door. The brute went after him, leaving the gun on the floor where it lay. This guy didn't figure he needed any weapons other than his hands and feet. Blakelock was inclined to agree with him. He staggered to his feet and ran for the study, feeling his attacker's presence closing behind him.

One of the biggest mistakes people make in a fight is that they strike once or twice and then back off. Blakelock knew that even against a monster like this guy, his only chance was an explosive barrage coming at him from all angles. So as he crossed the threshold, he grabbed the edge of the heavy pine door with his left hand and slammed it hard into the brute's face. Any normal man would have at least staggered. The brute grunted and kept coming. So did Blakelock.

He delivered a hard front kick just below the guy's kneecap. He let his foot touch the floor and stepped in for a second kick, driven by terror and desperation, right into the guy's balls. That made his face flush, so he did it again, and that made him pause. The short pause was all Blakelock needed to step back and grab the marble top from the lamp table beside the filing cabinets. He swung it hard, putting his whole body into it, not giving a damn where it landed. It struck him in the upper arm, gashing his muscle and making him wheeze.

The next blow was instinctive. He knew the brute would come for him. So instead of swinging the marble top back-handed, he smashed it straight up into the giant's face. It struck his upper lip and his nose with the combined force of Blakelock's thrust and the brute's own lunge. Blood erupted from his nostrils and his ruptured lips. Two teeth fell to the floor smeared in gore. Blakelock didn't pause. He raised the slab of marble over his head. The brute raised his arms as a reflex to ward off the blow, and Blakelock smashed his right instep into his testicles for the third time. The brute bent double, and his knees began to sag. And Blakelock brought the heavy slab crashing down onto the back of his head. The man grunted and fell forward.

Blakelock staggered back to the bedroom and retrieved his Glock. By the time he had returned to the study, the man was on his hands and knees. Blakelock put four rounds into the back of his head and sprayed his brains across the tiled floor. The body fell awkwardly, half across its own arms, and Blake-lock put another five rounds into his heart. It paid to be sure with brutes.

After that, he went through his pockets but found only a steel flash drive with a ring at one end. He looked down at the mangled body and held up the drive. "That's it? Just this?"

He spent the next hour scouring the house, pausing only to pour himself a large whiskey to steady the shaking in his hands. It was as he was draining the glass that he noticed the pool had become illuminated automatically as night had fallen. The seed of a thought came to him. He put down the heavy crystal tumbler and walked out to the turquoise glow.

The warped, black objects were at the bottom, at the deep end.

"Son of a bitch..."

He stripped and took a dive, swam down to the bottom, and collected up the shattered drives. They were probably beyond rescuing, but the nerds at ODIN might be able to get something from them. He erupted to the surface, clambered out, dried himself and dressed, then dumped the laptop and the hard drive, along with the shattered bits of external drive, in the trunk of his car. After that, he dressed, made his way back to the Merc, and headed back toward Mahon. As he wound his way through the blackness of the tunnel of trees, he called ODIN, was put through voice recognition, and finally heard Nero's voice on the other end.

"I hope you have good news for me."

"It's a mixed bag, sir. Yasha Orlev had been tortured and killed when I got there. It looked like he knew it was coming because it seems he smashed all his external drives and dumped them in his swimming pool."

"That is unfortunate."

"Having said that, there was a desktop computer in his office and also a laptop. I have both of them. It is just possible he didn't get around to wiping them."

"Good, a forlorn hope but hope nonetheless."

"Also, his killer was still in the house."

"The fact that you are talking to me without dropping heavy hints about your personal safety heartens me."

"I killed him, sir, and found a flash drive in his pocket. I am on my way back to Mahon right now. I'll make up my travel plans as I go. We don't know who else is on the island."

"I agree. Keep me posted."

"Will do, sir."

He hung up and drove on through the dark tunnel of trees into the blackness of the night with an increasing sense of uncertainty.

ONE

The rain was torrential. The spray rose two feet off the road, obscuring the wheels of the cars creeping down Rhode Island Avenue toward Logan Circle. At one point I was pretty sure I saw a large, wooden ark bobbing along five or six cars ahead, but it was hard to be sure because of the mist. That got me thinking about the animals going into the ark two by two—a story that is even more controversial than Darwin's theory of evolution—which in turn got me wondering about the western whiptail lizards, which are all female. Apparently they reproduce by a process called parthenogenesis. Parthenogenesis involves putting on some Barry White, breaking open the Bollinger and the oysters, getting close and friendly, and then cloning yourself.

So how many of those did Noah put on the ark? Just one, and *Playboy* for lizards?

Having advanced maybe fifteen feet, I got to wondering if the human race was evolving toward parthenogenesis and men would soon become redundant in a world of women who renounced makeup and refused to shave their legs and armpits. I decided that line of thought was not helpful or uplifting and turned on the radio.

"The question more and more people are asking—and note that I am actually risking prosecution by raising this point —the question more and more *Jews* are asking is, can it be true that the safest place for a Jew, after all these centuries, after all the massacres, after the Third Reich, the safest place for a Jew in this world is now actually Israel at war? A country six times smaller than New York State, surrounded on all sides by crazy people who want to annihilate the Jewish race, is *safer* than New York, Boston, Los Angeles, San Francisco, London, Paris, Berlin..."

The interviewer interrupted the speaker claiming he was exaggerating.

"Really? You think I'm exaggerating? You want to explain to me how it is that since October 7th, when over a thousand Israelis were murdered, raped, tortured, and abducted, all her allies have steadily turned against her? You want to explain to me how it is that Jews are no longer safe on the streets of New York? You want to explain to me how it is that Israel's major allies are now refusing to sell her arms...?"

The rain turned from torrential to deluge. I put my wipers on full, but all they did was add to the confusion caused by the inch-thick layer of rain on the windshield. The radio crackled and started playing a medley of Mozart, *Dark Side of the Moon*, and an ad for breakfast cereal.

I switched off the radio and turned carefully into 6th Street North West and, as the rain eased a little, I turned right into Q Street. I stopped outside the oxblood place on the corner with all the white stucco and saw the front door open and Aila Gallin walk down the steps and stroll across the garden like it was a refreshing shower on a warm April day.

"What they don't get," she said as she climbed in, demonstrating a telepathic link with both me and my car radio, "is"—she pulled the door closed and wiped the water from her eyes and face—"when we are annihilated, when we are wiped off the face of the planet, when they finally get rid of us, who is going to protect *them?*"

"The answer to that question is an opinion I am not allowed to share," I said as I pulled away.

"You just said it all. Say no more. You just summed it up. This world is going bat-shit crazy. They think—" She paused to stare at me and poke at the windshield. "They think that *they* are protecting *us*. What they don't realize is that they are *supposed* to be helping *us* protect *them*. We are the front line in a war, an all-out assault against democracy and everything and anything good humanity has ever achieved. We are all that stands between them and the Dark Ages. You abandon the front line at your peril."

"Good morning, Gallin."

"What's good about it?"

"I had eggs, bacon, English sausages, freshly baked wholegrain bread, and black coffee. That was good. And Manny Pacquiao sat on my lap and ate my bacon."

She lowered at me for a few seconds. "Manny Pacquiao is your cat, right?"

"Yeah, but he has never sat on my lap."

"He was a boxer."

"Probably the best ever, and a devoted student of Bruce Lee's Jeet Kune Do."

"You know what we need? We need another flood. Start over."

"You may get your wish if this keeps up. You and I might be the only survivors." I glanced at her. "What would our kids be like?"

She looked at me, but she didn't answer for a count of six —if you try it you'll see it's a long time. Then she said, "If they're lucky, they'll have my looks and my brains. You have a nice nose, though."

"Thanks."

"It would be a shame to break it. What does Nero want?"

"He refused to tell me anything over the phone."

The rain began to ease and with it the traffic, and after just over half an hour, we walked into Nero's office on Wilson Boulevard. As Nero and I exchanged good mornings, Gallin scowled at him.

"How come," she said without preamble, "I am seconded to you when the United States and the United Kingdom are reviewing their sale of arms to Israel? What is this? You get to use me, but I don't get to use you?"

Nero laced his fingers over the ample globe of his belly and regarded her first along his large nose and then from under his brows.

"First, Captain Gallin, I am not responsible for the stupidity of our political leaders. Second, the Five Eyes does not represent any one of the signatory countries. Third, Israel is an unofficial sixth eye, and fourth, if you have any slender chance of reversing this tide of stupidity that is engulfing the Western World, it is by operating through ODIN. Have you any more angry though relevant questions for me before we get down to business?"

"No."

"Then be seated and kindly refrain from speaking until you are able to talk sense."

She sat and said, "Can I have a coffee?"

"You can, Captain Gallin, and you may." He gestured me to sit, buzzed Lovelock, and told her to bring in coffee and pastries. Then he leaned back in his chair and said, "There is a flash drive. Last week, only three human beings on the planet knew precisely what was on it: myself, Professor David Geller, and a man called Yasha Orlev. Now only I know."

I said, "The other two are dead?"

"Yasha Orlev was killed yesterday at his home in Menorca. Tortured first and then killed."

"Do we know who by?"

"By whom? No. Peter Blakelock was on the job. He tracked him to The Balearic Islands and drove to his house. There, from what little he was able to tell me on the telephone, he found his body. He had toothpicks under his nails and had been stabbed in the heart. It seems Orlev may have been expecting the worst because, according to Peter, he had smashed all his external drives and thrown them in the deep end of his swimming pool."

Gallin said, "That speaks of desperation."

"Indeed. The need for effective speed. However, he said that he had found a desktop computer and a laptop and had them both. There was a small chance that Orlev had not yet gotten around to wiping them."

Gallin said, "Unlikely."

"Agreed, but an outside chance nonetheless. Peter then told me that the killer was still in the house, but he had managed to kill him. In his pocket he had found a flash drive. We must assume that Yasha Orlev had put all of his significant research onto the drive, wiped or destroyed everything else, and was intending to flee when his executioner arrived."

Gallin took over, and Nero arched an eyebrow at her as she said, "He put toothpicks under his nails until he told him where the flash drive was and then stabbed him in the heart."

"Thank you, Captain Gallin, I couldn't have expressed it better if you'd allowed me to. Peter told me he was making travel plans to return to Washington. I have had people looking out for him."

"But he has disappeared."

"You must be telepathic, Captain."

The door opened, and Lovelock came in looking dark and exquisite and smelling of lilacs. She put a silver tray of coffee on the desk along with a basket of hot croissants, winked at me, and left.

Gallin reached for a croissant while Nero poured coffee. I said, "So the key item here is the flash drive."

"Correct."

"What is on it that makes it so important?"

"I can't tell you."

"You said you were the only person who knew, now that Orlev was dead."

He handed Gallin a cup of coffee and another to me. "That is correct, Alex, but the contents are so sensitive that I cannot share them even with you and the captain. However, I shall tell you what I can."

He sat stirring his coffee for so long I began to wonder if that was it, he had told us all he could, but eventually he took a deep breath and sipped his coffee. As he set the cup down, he started to talk.

"Yasha Orlev had a very close friend. They had been close for over twenty years. This friend was Professor David Geller."

Gallin's eyebrow went up. "The professor at Tel Aviv University?"

"The very same, a world eminence in anthropology, social sciences, and psychology with an honorary doctorate in Chaos Theory from the University of London. Their relationship defied definition. At times they lived together, at other times they lived apart. Professor Geller was married twice..." He waved his hand in the air. "The mysteries of their relationship do not concern us. The fact is that they were very close friends, and by all accounts, that is all they were. They were not homosexuals.

"They often worked together. I am aware of three books they co-wrote, and they often researched subjects together, though the subsequent allocation of credit was not an issue. Yasha told me on one occasion that they were both more interested in the results of the research than in the credit given.

"In 2022 I spoke to David Barnea at the Mossad about some concerns I had. What they were is irrelevant to this conversation, but we agreed that the University of Tel Aviv should approach Professor Geller and ask him to conduct some research..." He trailed off, picked up a croissant, and slowly broke it in half. "I cannot disclose the exact nature of the research, though in general terms, I can tell you that it concerns the drift of democratic Western civilization—and I use the term democratic in the widest possible sense—the drift, as I say, toward a totalitarian, tyrannical dystopia."

I said, "Wow" with my mouth full of croissant, so it came out more like "Womph!"

Nero arched an eyebrow at me and said, "A valuable contribution, Alex, thank you."

"I mean," I said and swallowed, "that's a pretty unusual thing for the Mossad to be researching."

Gallin was shaking her head, but Nero answered. He said, "Not as much as you might think. If you said MI5 or the Secret Intelligence Service, the French DGSE, or the Australian Secret Intelligence Service"—he waved his hand in the air—"or any number of other secret services, I would agree. But there are two exceptions to that rule, Alex."

I could see Gallin nodding at her third croissant. I said, "The Mossad and who else?"

Gallin spoke with a mouth full of croissant but managed to articulate, "The Mossad and the CIA."

"Thank you, Captain, that is precisely right. These are the two Western nations, Israel and the United States, who will be most deeply impacted by this trend. The United States because of her position, since the Third Reich, as global policeman, and Israel..." He trailed off and shook his head. "Israel partly because she is a lone democracy beset on all sides by hostile totalitarian tyrannies and partly because whenever the world drifts toward darkness, the Jewish people seem to become the first victims. You can almost set your clock by it." He held up three fingers. "Three signs: first free speech is curtailed, second people start burning books, and third, they start persecuting Jews." He turned to Gallin. "Am I wrong? Tell me if I am wrong."

"You're not wrong. You're right."

"Thank you. I am no fan of the methods employed by Central Intelligence, but their objectives are, usually, sound. So the CIA and the Mossad keep a very close watch on these trends. And since nine-eleven, both agencies have been aware of a drift toward a somewhat dystopian totalitarianism. " He paused, hesitated a moment, and added as an aside, "Not only in the East. When Mr. Obama started flirting with Iran and encouraging their nuclear program, alarm bells sounded in Tel Aviv and in many departments of Central Intelligence. So David Geller was commissioned to conduct some in-depth research into this trend and advise, to the best of his considerable abilities, whether this was simply part of a pendulum swing that would correct itself or whether it was part of a long-term trend. If the latter was the case, he was asked to identify what was causing that trend."

Gallin said, "And the first thing he did was turn to his long-time friend Yasha Orlev to help him in his research."

"Correct."

I said, "So I gather that Geller and Orlev's findings are contained on that flash drive."

Nero sighed heavily. "That is a totally unwarranted assumption, Alex; however, it is quite correct also."

I scratched my chin. "Let me make another totally unwarranted assumption. The fact that we have only spoken about Yasha Orlev, except when it came to who commissioned the report from whom, is down to the fact that Professor Geller didn't die of natural causes. He was also murdered."

He blinked at me. "It is too flimsy to be called analysis. However, your intuition is correct, Alex."

"Thank you, sir. What do we know about his murder?"

He grunted. At almost three hundred pounds, a grunt from Nero was an event. "Not very much, I'm afraid. Not unlike Karl Marx, they decided the ideal cities from which to study this phenomenon were London and New York"—he

spread out his hands and pushed out his bottom lip—
"arguably one city divided by an ocean. Orlev was based in
New York, and Geller was based in London. It was convenient
for them. Orlev had established himself in the United States,
and Geller had easy access from London to his home in Tel
Aviv."

I glanced at Gallin. "Did your father have contact with
him?"

She shook her head. "Not as far as I am aware."

Nero was also shaking his head. "Not at all. This was very
compartmentalized. He was incognito, and his research and his
presence were kept extremely low key."

"So theoretically at least, very few people knew he was
there, and even fewer knew what he was there *for*."

"As a starting point, those are valid premises, yes."

He took a deep breath and leaned back in his chair. I had
never really seen Nero look haggard, but in that moment, that
was exactly how he looked. And that was the first real indication I had of just how bad the situation was.

"Let me describe the events of his murder for you, and then
I shall tell you exactly what I want from you."

TWO

HE POURED HIMSELF A CUP OF COFFEE, LEANED BACK in his large, leather chair, and sipped. He didn't put the cup down. He held it between the pudgy forefinger and thumb of each hand.

"David Geller's body was found in the apartment he shared with Yasha Orlev in London's Notting Hill Gate whenever Orlev was in town. The apartment was on the sixth floor of a block on Kensington Church Street. He was found last Friday, November 8th, at eleven-fifteen in the morning. There is no precise time of death; as you both know, that is almost impossible to fix."

I asked, "When was he last seen?"

"Wednesday the 6th, somewhere around half past nine or ten in the evening, by his cleaner."

Gallin said, "So he was shot sometime between ten p.m. November the 6th and eleven a.m. November 8th. About thirty-seven hours."

"Correct. The only access to the apartment was through

the front door. The exterior offers no means of scaling the façade, and there is no access to a terrace or a balcony from above. However, there was no forced entry, the lock was undamaged, and Geller was sitting on his sofa facing the television, which was on, with a bullet hole in his right temple. There was an exit wound just below his left temple. There was a great deal of gore on the left side of the sofa, a genuine Arne Vodder, and the lead slug was there, among the gore."

Gallin asked, "Was the weapon found?"

"Kindly control your impulse to interrupt. I am coming to that, and you may be sure I will cover all of the details.

"A nine millimeter casing was found on the carpet and, somewhat bizarrely, there was a Staccato P semi-automatic lying on the coffee table. Ballistics report that this was the gun that fired the slug that was found on the sofa and struck the casing that was found on the floor. It is the gun that was used to kill David Geller. It was not registered, and we have not as yet been able to trace the owner.

"In terms of fingerprints found in the apartment, there were those you would expect: Geller himself, Yasha Orlev, the cleaner, and the landlady. There was another set which we are running through all the databases available to the Five Eyes, but so far with no success."

Gallin gave a shrug. "So the killer rang at the door and was admitted voluntarily. We have to assume that his killer knew that Geller would be alone. Both facts suggest Geller knew his killer and was not afraid of him. Also, Geller was obviously comfortable and at home with his killer because the guy is standing there in the middle of the floor while Geller is watching TV. Then this guy pulls his Staccato and shoots him. One single, clean shot. He's used to using a gun, and killing a man doesn't upset him. At least not enough to make his hand tremble."

"That is an accurate summary of what happened."

I was frowning. "What about Orlev?"

"I am coming to that. He was in Cornwall. Your questions at this point add nothing to the data I am giving you. It is not clear—and this is very important—it is not clear whether anything was taken. There were no signs of robbery in the conventional sense. His money, his wallet, his credit cards were all untouched. On the face of it, his killer simply arrived, shot him, placed the gun on the coffee table, and left."

Gallin was scratching her head. "So nothing was taken—"

Nero plowed on, "*However!*" He paused, eying her from under his brows. "All of Professor Geller's research, his laptop, all his external drives and his handwritten notes were gone."

I spread my hands. "So this flash drive of Orlev's...?"

He nodded. "It gets complicated, Alex. About a week before he was killed, he called Orlev and told him he felt uneasy and thought there might be somebody watching him, and he handed Orlev a flash drive which he claimed contained all of his research."

Gallin snapped, "How do you know this?"

Nero arched an eyebrow at her and said reluctantly, "That is an excellent and very pertinent question, Captain. And the answer is, I don't. Yasha Orlev contacted me two days before Professor Geller's murder and told me that the professor had met with him in Notting Hill, where they had had this exchange, and Professor Geller had given him the flash drive."

"Sweet Jesus."

"I'm afraid he won't help us."

I asked, "Have you seen what's on the flash drive?"

He shook his head. "I have only Orlev's word." He paused. "And he is dead, so his word has no value. It had little value when he was alive. Now it has none."

I repressed a scowl and didn't do a great job of it. "Sir, you have to tell us what's on the drive. Our whole strategy —"

"*Out of the question!*" He yelled it. It was the first time I had ever seen Nero yell. He did it twice. "*Out of the question! Not negotiable!*" He raised a finger. "*Do not argue. The answer is no!*" He slammed his palm down on the desk and made a lot of noise. "*No!*"

I spread my hands. "I don't see how—"

"We shall come to that, should you and the captain *ever* stop interrupting me!"

Silence fell on the room. It didn't have much choice. Nero took a deep breath and flipped a switch on his desk. "Lovelock, be kind enough to bring in a bottle of Bollinger, very cold." He flipped the switch again and said, "Forgive me. This case is affecting my nerves."

I waited a moment before telling him, "It's having the same effect on mine."

He gave me a size one smile—really thin—and told me, "Then I recommend a glass of very cold champagne. It always works for me. Perspective, you know. The question now is, what do I need from you? Put another way, what am I asking you to do?"

Gallin nodded. "Yes, sir, what exactly are you asking us to do?"

He gazed at the edge of his desk for a long while and touched it with his fingertips.

"First and foremost, it is absolutely imperative—I cannot stress how important it is—that you recover that flash drive.

There is a possibility that Orlev lied to me, but I do not think so. I think, for reasons I cannot share, I think what he had was the genuine drive. It is utterly imperative that you recover it. Second, and of only slightly less importance, find who killed him and find out who they worked for..." He paused, and his eyes became hooded. "Use whatever means are necessary. It could not be more important."

The door opened, and Lovelock came in with a bucket of ice, three frosted glasses, and a bottle of Bollinger. He took the bottle and waved her away. She made a face at me and left.

As he struggled with the wire, I asked, "You said Professor Geller was married?"

"Yes. She is in Tel Aviv. Marian Geller. Captain Gallin will be able to guide you there, but I doubt she will be very helpful —" He paused and stared at Gallin. "Mrs. Geller, not you."

"I gathered. So Geller had his place in London and his home with his wife in Tel Aviv, and Orlev had his place in New York and another place in Menorca, in the Balearic Islands."

"That is correct."

"Professor Geller was killed at his apartment in London, and Orlev was killed at his villa in Menorca."

"Yes."

"Geller was executed by somebody he knew, with a single shot to the head, and Orlev was tortured and killed with a single knife to the heart. Both killings reek of pro." She turned to me. "We need to go and talk to Geller's wife."

I gave two small shrugs, one with my shoulders and the other with my eyebrows. "Any particular reason?"

"Yeah. Because she's his wife."

I offered another shrug to Nero, who was sipping champagne. He shook his head as he set down his glass. "In a universe where logic clings on by its fingernails, sometimes it is wise to listen to women. We, as men, are in touch with reality. They are in touch with truth."

"I'll try to remember that. Unless there is anything else we need to know, I think we should probably be making a move."

He narrowed his eyes at me. "I was in fact wondering why you were still here."

Only the faintest shadow of a twitch at the corner of his mouth told me it was a joke.

IN THE CAR, headed back through what was now a steady, gray drizzle, I got as far as "So…" before she started talking.

"This…" She made circles with her left index finger. "This *relationship* between Geller and Orlev, what's that about?"

"Often I am able to understand you by telepathic osmosis. But not this time. What, in fact, is your question?"

She looked away at the passing houses, the drizzle and the umbrellas, like she had decided it wasn't worth talking to me. Then she said, "I mean" and turned to narrow her eyes at me. "Women are complex. We have a richer hormonal make-up than you have. Relationships between women can go very deep and remain purely emotional. That initial bonding we have with our mothers endures throughout life. In psychoanalysis, they try to understand it by contrasting the Electra complex with the Oedipus complex, but Freud himself, who was an extremely honest man, admitted before dying that he had never managed to understand women. We are *very* complex."

"Oh." I nodded. "Thank you. I didn't know that."

"I am not listening to you." She shook her head. "But guys?

You are not complex. Guys are all straight lines. 'Can I have sex with it without having to marry it?' 'Is it worth marrying to have sex with it?' 'Should I shoot it or keep it as a pet?'—You get the metaphor. They are all basically the same question. With guys, there are two basic states: penetrate or don't penetrate."

"That is pretty insulting, Gallin."

"I know. But I am talking on a very basic level. So when guys become gay, they try to become more complex, but really, instead, they just become much more sensitive. Which is why gay men seem much more feminine than straight women, because they are trying much harder, but it *still* comes down to the same thing. Women don't have two basic states. We have *lots* of basic states. So my point is that relationship that Nero described between Orlev and Geller? I don't get it. It is too complex for two men."

I spent a while nodding slowly at the gray road ahead. Finally I said, "My impulse is to tell you you are talking a lot of bullshit and then ask you what I have done to annoy you."

"See?" She gestured at me with her left hand as she looked right, out of the window. "That's a perfect example."

"However, I am going to remember what Nero said: 'In a universe where logic clings on by its fingernails, sometimes it is wise to listen to women. We, as men, are in touch with reality. They are in touch with truth.' So I am going to shut up and be open to the possibility that you actually know what you're talking about."

She didn't say anything, so I added, "Having said that, I protest at the implication that I am some Neanderthal whose mind is solely occupied with the possibility of getting laid."

"That's not what I meant."

"Well, it might surprise you to know that I am fully aware of the complex dimensions of our relationship."

She frowned at me. "You are?"

I drove in silence for a while, then shook my head. "No. I have this recurring fantasy—or what your friend Freud would call a phantasy—with a PH—that one day we'll get drunk and hit the sack."

"Who, you and Freud? You know he's dead, right?"

"Funny. You're funny. Really. So getting back on track, you think the relationship between Geller and Orlev was too complex to be male? You said gay men are just as simple as straight ones. So where does that leave you?"

"I don't know. Clearly they weren't women, and clearly they weren't gay. So what?"

I shrugged. "If there is any logic to what you are saying, which I seriously doubt, the only other option is that their relationship was more than just a friendship."

She stared at me. "More than just a friendship. What would that be?"

"If it wasn't sexual, it would have greater professional depth than was apparent. Like Einstein and Niels Bohr, Einstein and Schrödinger would be a better example, or Oppenheimer. Or, in a completely different field, Van Gogh and Paul Gauguin."

"Where that drive to penetrate becomes a shared search for some kind of truth."

She said it to herself. So I didn't bother to answer because I thought she was leading herself down a blind alley. She must have read my mind because she gave me that look like I was an idiot.

"He's married. Professor Geller is married. He makes a lot

of money, and he lives on Danin Street, in one of the best areas in the city. He is a genius and also a top academic, and the Mossad commission from him a report on the drift in Western civilization away from democracy toward totalitarianism. And to conduct that research, he moves to London. I mean that, right there, makes no sense to me at all."

I nodded because she was right. She went on.

"And it makes even less sense when you bring in Yasha Orlev, who is supposedly helping him in his research, unacknowledged, almost halfway around the world on another continent. You know," she said with heavy sarcasm, "where they can meet over breakfast for a chat about their latest findings."

I shrugged. "They were academics. Academics are weird, to say the least, and there are things like Facetime, Zoom, Skype…"

She grunted. I added, "And if they were in some Bohemian, gay relationship, they would both have gone to London or both to New York."

"That is kind of my point. What's the deal here? Have you ever, *ever* met an academic who was willing to do vital research and not be acknowledged for it?"

"No," I admitted, "but neither have I met two academics who were jointly commissioned a frankly bizarre piece of research by ODIN and the Mossad and who were both murdered within a few days of each other. Also, most academics are intelligent, but only a few are real geniuses. Or would Nero call them genii?"

She didn't answer, but this time it was a silence that said she agreed with me. So I went on.

"It's hard to know where our starting point is here. Do we

approach this as a double murder of two men engaged in a weird relationship and hope the killer will lead us to the...” I spread my hands. “The *truth?* Or do we try and pump your dad and find out at least what the Mossad know, think they know, suspect, whatever, that led them to commission this research?”

She took a deep breath. “That—*that*—would be the right starting point, but I know my dad, and he would never give out intelligence that was classified. Not even to me.”

I turned into Q Street and pulled up outside her house. We stared at each other a moment, and I said: “Then call him, explain the situation, and tell him to ask for permission to read us in. It’s as much in their interest as in ours.”

She nodded. “Yeah, OK. But no guarantee, Mason.”

“I know that. Pick you up in an hour and a half?”

“And have another ride in this hearse? No way, big guy. I’ll pick you up in a real car. We’ll do twice the distance in half the time.”

She climbed out and crossed the sidewalk with her hands in her pockets like the sun was shining and the birds were singing. By the time she put the key in the door and pushed it open, her shoulders were sodden and her hair was like wet rats’ tails. She smiled and winked as she closed the door. It gave me a nice warm feeling, and I drove off toward Adams Street with a smile on my face.

THREE

We touched down at Tel Aviv's Ben Gurion airport at eleven a.m. in ODIN's Gulfstream. We picked up our rental car from Hertz and drove straight to Danin Street. Gallin took the wheel, and I sat and watched a blurred, weaving version of Tel Aviv as it became a living example of Einstein's General Theory of Relativity.

"Did you call her and tell her we were on our way?"

"Yup."

"How did she sound?"

"Like her husband had recently been murdered."

"That's not helpful, Gallin."

"She sounded upset but like she was wanting to help." After a moment, she added, "Don't be sensitive. I am not mad at you. I'm mad at Geller and Orlev."

I screwed up my face. "What? Why?"

"I don't know yet. They were playing some stupid game." She gestured at the road ahead with her upturned palm, like she was offering me a hologram of what was in her mind. "He's supposed to be in London keeping a low profile or some bull-shit. But he knows his killer, and his killer knows he's alone. How does that work? They were playing some kind of stupid, dangerous game."

We turned into Danin Street, and she skidded to a halt and killed the engine. She stared at me with no expression. "Be nice. Be sensitive."

"Cut it out, will you, Gallin!"

We climbed out and made for the house.

Mrs. Geller opened the door before we arrived. I guess the shock was that she was young and beautiful. She was probably in her mid thirties, though she could pass for late twenties. Her skin was flawless and on the bronze side of brown. Her hair was blue-black and tied back in a loose ponytail, and her eyes were a startling deep blue. She glanced at me but turned her attention to Gallin.

"Are you Captain Aila Gallin?" Her accent was slightly American with a hint of exotic.

"Yes, Mrs. Geller. This is my colleague Alex Mason. He is with United States Intelligence. May we come in?"

She stood back and said, "Please. I've made coffee. I can make something else if you prefer."

We told her coffee would be fine, and she led us through to a large, over-stuffed living room which was littered with books and magazines and newspapers. A set of sliding glass doors stood open onto a large, bountiful, messy lawn rich with roses and wildflowers, framed by dense trees.

There was a heavy, ethnic coffee table set in the midst of two huge armchairs and a huge sofa. On the table there was a silver tray with a coffeepot, cream, sugar, and three cups.

Mrs. Geller lowered herself carefully onto the sofa, like she was afraid she might break if she went too fast. Her back and neck were rigid, and her hands were pressed into her lap. She stared at me for the longest five seconds of my life, and I watched tears well in her eyes. I glanced at Gallin, but she just sat forward and said, "I'll pour the coffee. You take cream and sugar, Mrs. Geller?"

Her answer was barely a whisper. "Just cream, no sugar."

Gallin handed me a small, black coffee, then handed Mrs. Geller hers, and as she did so, she sat next to her and put her arm around her.

"We can come back another time."

The answer came without aggression or force, but with quiet strength. "No," she said. "We must strike while the iron is hot. Every minute that passes, the trail gets colder. What do you want to know?"

"Everything you know." Mrs. Geller nodded softly. Gallin said, "How much of his work did he share with you?"

"Not much. Nothing, really. A lot of it was pure math, which meant nothing to me."

I frowned at Gallin, and she frowned back at me. "Math?"

Mrs. Geller looked a little surprised. "Yes, David was a mathematician first, and then an anthropologist. He had a theory that it must be possible to predict the development of societies by the use of pure mathematics. He called it Chaos Theory." She paused and thought for a moment, gazing down at the sofa and running her hand gently over the calico upholstery. "He said societies were driven by binary forces: the negative force of needs like hunger, greed, and poverty, and the positive force of violence. He said that knowing that, he could develop equations to predict social models." She raised her shoulders an eighth of an inch. "I am making it sound very simplistic, but if you had heard him explain it…" She trailed off.

I smiled at her. "So in general terms, do you think it was accurate to say he was engaged in a mathematical analysis of social dynamics?"

She gave another small shrug. "Yes, I suppose so."

"I want you to understand something, Mrs. Geller. It is absolutely and totally against the law for a person holding classified information to share it with anyone who has no clearance." I paused, and Gallin scowled at me. I ignored her and went on. "But it is not against the law to receive that information. So if Professor Geller shared with you anything about the work he was commissioned to do, he may have been wrong to do that, but you were not at fault, and you can tell us about it."

It was hard to read her expression, but there was something of embarrassment about it. "He… We, we didn't talk much." She smiled at me and then seemed to turn to Gallin for support. "You know, we had become comfortable, and we didn't have a lot of conversation. He would talk a lot to Yasha. Yasha Orlev, you know. They talked very much. Mostly on the telephone. They would call each other and talk for hours." She hesitated. "And then sometimes, especially after a telephone call, he would just talk—not *to* anyone. He would just talk, aloud, walking around the house. When he did that, I was not really sure how I was supposed to respond. But I don't think he noticed me anyway."

I smiled like I understood. "That's the way with geniuses, I guess. They are focused so hard on their own thoughts…" I trailed off, then said, "But I gather you tried to be supportive and engage with him at least up to a point."

She nodded. "Yes, I tried. I did try."

"So even if you didn't understand a lot of the terminology, you must have listened with care when he was talking. Does anything come to mind about what he said? Did anything strike you as odd or unusual? Were there names? Anything at all that stuck in your mind, even if it seems absurd to you now?"

She thought for a long while. "He did mention some names," she said at last. "Barak Hussein, he repeated that a lot, with a kind of bitterness. David used to feel things very intensely. Hussein..." She trailed off, her gaze lost in the back yard. "Jim, Mitch Hanson?" She glanced at me like she wanted me to tell her if she'd gotten it right. "And Kathleen, Ira Bellow, and a general, General William H. Drake. Could that be?"

I smiled. "That is very helpful, Mrs. Geller. We'll look into those names."

She screwed up her brow. "He also seemed to become obsessed with ancient Rome. He talked a lot about the emperor Nero, and he quoted Cicero a lot."

Gallin frowned. "Really? Can you remember the quote?"

Mrs. Geller laughed. "I don't think I shall ever forget it, he repeated it so many times." She thought for a moment with her gaze directed at the ceiling, "'A nation can survive its fools. It can even survive the ambitious, but it cannot survive treason from within. The enemy at the gates is less formidable, for he is known, and carries his banner openly. But the traitor moves freely among those within the gates, his sly whisper rustling through all the alleys, heard in the very halls of government itself.'"

She fell silent. Outside a bird called a single note but repeated it over and over. A car sighed as it passed.

Gallin said, "Did he ever say why he had that particular quote on his mind? Did you ever ask?"

She shook her head and looked down at her hands in her lap. After a moment, she smiled. Ironically, it was an expression that was full of sadness.

"If you betray the king, that is treason, and they are allowed to kill you for it. If you betray your family, there are all sorts of justifications for it, and the most you get is a divorce and alimony."

"Did David betray you, Mrs. Geller?"

She raised her face and met Gallin's eye. "I don't know, Captain. I often wondered." She shook her head. "He was not queer—we have to call it gay now, don't we—but he had no love or respect for women. He used to joke that when God offered Adam a partner, he told Adam it would cost him a kidney, an eye, one lung, and one of his arms, and at that point, Adam interrupted him and asked, 'What can you give me for a rib?'" She tried a laugh, and when we didn't join in, she went on. "He often said that, whatever God may have intended, we were not created equal, and life was too short to engage in limping conversations with an intellectually stunted gender. He said that more than once."

Gallin's eyebrows rose high on her forehead. "Wow."

"So his closest relationships were with men, especially with Yasha. But he was heterosexual, and I often wondered, when he was away…"

"Did you visit him while he was in London?" The question was subtle, but I knew where Gallin was going with it. Mrs. Geller's smile became rueful. "No, that would only have annoyed him. He said he needed to keep a low profile, and my presence would just make him more conspicuous. He phoned a couple of times, but aside from that, we had no contact." She gave a bark of a laugh. It came out too loud, and she clamped her hand over her mouth. "His last words to me," she said, "in this world were, 'I have to go.'" Her face crumbled, and she began to weep. "I have to go..."

Gallin put her arms around her and held her a while. As the sobbing subsided, she said quietly, "Were you with friends when it happened, when you found out?"

"They don't know exactly when it happened, do they? The man from the Institute came and told me. They searched the house for any notes he might have left behind. But he had taken everything with him. I'd been with my brother and his family for a few days. They called me, from the Institute, and I came back. They said he'd been shot. They said it was instant. He didn't suffer."

She patted Gallin's knee and smiled at her. "He was a difficult man. He was small, but in his own way, he was a giant. He was too big for a small world. He loved Israel. He died for Israel. Israel was his true wife."

A thought came into my mind and made me frown. "Did Yasha Orlev contact you? After this happened, did Yasha call you?"

She looked surprised at the question. "No. No, I had no contact with Yasha. We met a couple of times, but we were not friends."

"Sure. Mrs. Geller, I just want to go back to one point that might be important, and then we'll leave you in peace. You intimated that you thought Professor Geller might have been having an affair, or perhaps more than one." I waited a moment to see if she'd say anything. All she did was avert her eyes. I went on. "You said it was because he was heterosexual and had little respect for women. Forgive me, but that seems to me to be something of a leap. Was there anything more concrete?"

She took a long time to answer. Finally she took a deep breath and sighed loudly.

"David was not a good man at hiding things. He was too —" She seemed to bite back a word and started again. "He was too sure of himself, too proud ever to feel he needed to hide anything from anyone. So from comments he made over the years, I had come to suspect that he fairly regularly engaged in sexual intercourse with other women. At first it hurt, but over time, I got used to it. It was just organic relief with them, but he chose to marry me. That was what I told myself."

Gallin said, "But...?"

"But—it must have been a week or two, perhaps a little more, before he died—I ran into an acquaintance of ours, Natalya. Dr. Natalya Ivanova. She is an attractive woman, a professor of Russian history at the university, a colleague of David's. She is, like him, very intense and highly intelligent. Perhaps not as intelligent as she thinks!" There was a momentary flash of anger and even venom, but she quickly covered it with a laugh. "I remember it very vividly. She came running up to me in the supermarket." She fell suddenly into a startling mimicry, hunching her shoulders and shifting her hips, with her head on one side. "'Oh, Marian, poor you! How are you coping with David so far away? If you need *anything at all* do be sure and let me know. Though I won't be here the next couple of weeks. I'm flying to Kings College in London. I'll be visiting David if you want me to take him a message...'" She stopped, suddenly pale with anger, staring at an empty space above the coffee table. "I didn't even know his address in London. But she did. She was going to visit him."

Silence descended on the room for the second time. I saw Gallin draw breath and gave my head a microscopic shake. She caught it and pressed her lips together.

I said, "Mrs Geller, is there anyone you can think of who might be able to give us a more precise indication of what he was working on?"

"I don't know. Perhaps Natalya Ivanova. Perhaps they had pillow talk," she said bitterly, then shook her head. "But he would never betray Israel. He might betray me, but never Israel. Perhaps the vice president head of research, Professor Benjamin Glazerson. They were close, and David respected him." She gave a small shrug. "It's not my place, but I think he may have been David's link with the Mossad."

I nodded and made to stand. "I don't think we need trouble you anymore, Mrs. Geller. I am—we both are—very sorry for your loss. Thank you for you time and your patience."

Gallin got to her feet, but Mrs. Geller remained sitting for a moment. "My loss...?" Then she said, "If I think of anything else..." but left it hanging. She stood suddenly and led us to the door. She wished us well, and the door closed behind us.

Gallin climbed behind the wheel. I got in beside her and slammed the door.

"We have to be aware, Mason," she said to her hands which were resting on the wheel, "that this might be one almighty unholy mess."

"You think so?"

"Geller's murder might have *absolutely nothing* to do with his research into civilization's drift toward dystopian tyranny and *everything* to do with Natalya Ivanova."

I sighed and grunted at the same time and said, "I would have to agree with you, Gallin." I turned to look at her and screwed up my face. "But a single shot to the temple at maybe ten or twelve feet? And *zero* forensic evidence? I don't see Marian Geller as capable of that. Her emotions are all over the place. A tiny shake firing a 9 mm semi-automatic could translate over twelve feet into a maybe total miss. This slug went right through his temple. And his killer was cool enough to know he'd done his job. It was a single shot, and he left the gun on the coffee table. Then left. Can you see Marian Geller doing that?"

She shook her head and pushed out her lower lip. "I don't know, Mason. I don't know what ten years of marriage to a man like Geller can do to a woman. Maybe we were, just now" —she gestured back toward the house—"the audience to an Oscar-winning performance."

"You have a point, Gallin. We shouldn't lose sight of the fact that she had a powerful motive, and there was no hiding her bitterness."

She nodded. "Hell hath no fury like a woman scorned, Mason. And she had learned to really *hate* her husband." I glanced at her, surprised at the strength of the word hate. She fired up the engine and underscored it. "That was *hatred* in her eyes. Make no mistake."

And she pulled away.

FOUR

WE MADE OUR WAY TO ARLOZOROV STREET, THEN
headed west toward the Hilton, where Lovelock had booked us
a suite. On the way, Gallin made a call. She spoke briefly in
Hebrew, but I caught the words "...vice president head of
research, Professor Benjamin Glazerson..." a few more curt
phrases, and she hung up.

"What was that?"

"I called the office and told them I wanted to talk to the
vice president head of research, Professor Benjamin Glazerson
at TAU." She glanced at me. "That's Tel Aviv University."

"Yeah, I got that."

"I also told them I wanted to talk to Natalya Ivanova. If I
just call up, they are going to give me the runaround, at least
Natalya is, but if the office calls first, we are pretty much guar-
anteed an interview."

"Nice."

"Right. That right there is the slide toward a totalitarian

dystopia. So hotel, shower, change of clothes, lunch, and in the afternoon we talk to these two characters."

I gave my head a little twitch. "An in-depth chat with Professor Glazerson could be very illuminating, but I know already what he's going to say. He is going to tell us what Nero told us: 'Take a hike, this is classified above top secret.'"

"Maybe, but not necessarily. Either way, my money is on the Russian lover—assuming she's still among the living. I'm telling you"—she waved a finger at me—"it is not beyond the bounds of possibility that Natalya Ivanova became the straw that broke Mrs. Geller's back..."

She paused and frowned. I smiled and nodded. "Isn't it sad when bad things happen to good metaphors?"

"You know what I mean. He was just rubbing her face in it: 'I own you, and I can do what I like with you!' She snapped, got a flight to London, and bam." She waved her hand at me. "I know what you said before. You can't see her being that cold and efficient, but guys are schmucks when it comes to beautiful '*vulnerable*' women." She made inverted commas with her fingers. "And cold rage can do weird things to a person. That's why they call it *cold* rage. See?"

"Yes, I see. I had never thought of that," I said. "But what about Menorca? Did she then fly over there and stick tooth-picks under Yasha Orlev's fingernails before stabbing him in the heart with a kitchen knife? And if so, what did she hope to achieve?"

She grunted, and as we pulled in to the hotel and moved through the barriers, she said, "This is not straightforward, Mason. Lots of things come together here. It's like a Chinese puzzle."

"Sure, and one of those things is the contents of the flash

drive. It is so damned sensitive Nero won't even tell *us* about it." I shook my head. "This was a professional hit, Gallin. Mrs. Geller has to be considered, but she'll turn out to be a wild goose chase."

So we checked in, showered, changed our clothes and had lunch, and as Gallin drained the last of her beer and wiped her mouth with the back of her wrist, her cell rang. She leaned back in her chair, belched softly, and put the phone to her ear.

"Yeah." She listened for a moment and smiled at me. "Yes, Professor, I am Captain Aila Gallin. I would very much like to talk to you." She listened again and started shaking her head. "Not over the telephone, Professor." She frowned. "You did say that the director had telephoned you?" She listened, then gave a small shrug. "He did, so what exactly is the problem?" Another short pause. "Oh, good. Say in twenty minutes?" She hesitated a moment, then added, "Professor, I had hoped to speak with Dr. Natalya Ivanova today as well... She's still in London? No, that's fine. We'll talk about it when you get here... The Hilton."

She hung up.

I drummed my fingers on the table and winced. "That is a long time to be still in London."

"You think your professional hit man took her out too, before flying to the Balearic Islands?"

I scratched my chin. "Meeting up with Geller might have been secondary. She might actually have gone for work. What was she, Russian history?"

"Yeah. He'll tell us about her when he gets here. I've booked a small conference room. Let's go. I'll have reception send him up."

"Boy, you are on fire, kid. Have them send up some coffee too, will you?"

Professor Benjamin Glazerson was as good as his word and was shown into our small conference room twenty-five minutes later. He was probably five-ten but managed to look much shorter because he was so thin. His clothes—a tweed jacket, a collarless shirt and a pair of Levis—were probably expensive but managed to look cheap because they seemed to be too big for him, like they were hand-me-downs from his bigger brother, or he'd gotten wet and shrunk recently and hadn't got around to buying new clothes. His complexion was dark, and he peered from small eyes behind very large glasses.

Gallin was standing over by the window, and I got to my feet as he came in. He stopped and stared at us both, first Gallin and then me. I gestured to a chair. "Professor, thank you so much for coming. Will you sit and have some coffee?"

He approached the table, sat, and helped himself. "There's no point," he said as he poured, and I was surprised to hear a New York accent. "No point in thanking me. I would not have come, but you left me no choice." He looked at Gallin. "Are you Captain Gallin?" She nodded. "You pull some weight. I wouldn't have come, but I was *ordered* to come."

"Good to know." She approached and sat opposite him. "You can leave as soon as you like, after you've answered one question. What were the precise terms of the research you commissioned from Professor Geller? What was the precise title of his research?"

I wasn't surprised by her question. We had both come to the same conclusion: that whatever Nero said, we needed that information. He stared at her a moment, then turned to me. "What is this, an interrogation? Who are you? Are you CIA?"

I leaned forward with my elbows on the table and looked as pleasant as I knew how.

"You said you came because you were ordered to, Professor Glazerson. Did they order you to come and be an obstructive pain in the ass? Or did they order you to assist us in our investigation?"

He picked up his coffee and peered into it. "Disrespectful. Supposed to be our closest ally, but you come here like damned bullies—"

"Professor," I cut across him. "Respect is something you earn. Right now I have no respect for a man who is not prepared to lift a finger to protect his country. On the contrary. Instead of helping, you are being obstructive and evasive. And believe me, Professor, that will go in my report, and you can be damned sure it will go in Captain Gallin's report." I pointed at him. "You commissioned a report, the two men who undertook the research wound up murdered, and all you can do is whine about the fact that you are required to assist us in our investigation?"

Gallin said quietly, "That's a red flag right there."

He licked his lips, and his little eyes darted at Gallin from behind his heavy lenses. "You're Mossad."

"So what?"

"It was the Mossad who told me to commission the report in the first place. So ask them. What? They instructed you to come and find out what they already know?"

He wasn't wrong. Nero had not told us to find out what was on the flash drive. He wanted the flash drive itself. But we knew the only way we could find Geller and Orlev's killer and recover the drive was to identify our enemy, and the only way we could do that was by knowing what was on the damned drive.

Obviously I wasn't going to tell him that. Instead I said,

"Maybe you don't understand, Professor, but we don't need to explain or justify anything to you. We are here to ask you a question. You can choose not to answer, you can choose to be obstructive and give us a hard time. That is your choice, but if you know anything about the Mossad and the CIA, you also know that that would be a really bad idea."

Gallin cut in quietly before he could answer. "You got the call, Benjamin, answer the question. What were the precise terms of the research you commissioned from Professor Geller, and what was the precise title of his research?"

He shook his head, not in the negative but in disbelief. "Not Professor, not Doctor, not even mister. No please, no respect—"

She snarled, "Cut the bullshit and answer the damned question, *Benjamin!*"

He rubbed his face with his palms and refilled his cup. "It's not that simple."

I picked up my phone and set a timer. "You have ten minutes to make it simple. After that we leave and you are neck deep in shit, pal."

"First I am told never to tell anyone, on any account. Now I am told—"

Gallin slammed her hand on the table and shouted, "*Did you get the phone call?*"

"*Yes!*"

"*Then do it!*" He drew breath, but she interrupted him. "Circumstances have changed. Can't you see that? The two researchers are *dead! Murdered!* And their research has disappeared! There is no time for bullshit! Answer the question, Professor, or I swear I will *destroy you!*"

He took a while. He removed his glasses and rubbed the bridge of his nose. Somehow it made him more human.

"We provided a front. The university. We, the university, provided a front for the Mossad. I, for all intents and purposes, provided the general terms of the research. But the precise details were given to me by very senior officials. I don't know who."

I had a sinking feeling we were going to hear more of what we already knew, but I asked anyway.

"And those details?"

He sighed heavily and shook his head. Then he raised both hands, like we were holding a gun on him. "I am not saying this is what *I* think! This is what I was told to tell Professor Geller. This is *not* the opinion of the university."

"Cut to the chase."

"OK... The United States, the European Union, and the United Kingdom are governed by a cabal—"

"Bullshit!"

"I told you! I *told* you!"

Gallin said quietly, "Let's hear him out, Mason."

Glazerson eyed her curiously, then went on. "This cabal is not some group of thirteen men in black cloaks who sacrifice kids and drink their blood. A cabal is just a group who have a received wisdom. That is Kabbalah, received wisdom. This cabal was not named—not to me, at least—but what distinguishes them is that they have wealth and power beyond measure. They have the wealth and the power to shape the destiny of the human race—of the whole planet—but they are not elected. They do *not* hold public office. They are not subject to oversight, and they are not accountable to anybody. They got where they are by crushing opponents or by inheriting their position. They are true princes. They meet once or twice a year, and they make decisions about the destiny of the planet."

I was getting irritated and gave Gallin a look to let her know. She ignored me. I said, "This is Illuminati conspiracy theory crap, Glazerson. The Internet is full of this BS."

"I didn't say I believed it, Mason! I told you that. I said this was what I was *instructed* to brief Geller with. She threatened me if I didn't tell you, you would destroy me. So I'm telling you."

I sighed and sat back in my chair. "Fine. Should I go get some tin foil hats?"

He looked at Gallin and spread his hands. She gave me a look. "You done?" I blinked. She gave Glazerson the nod, and he went on.

"According to the people who briefed *me*, we are at a unique moment in history. There are eight point two *billion* people on the planet. At the turn of the millennium, just twenty-five years ago, it was six billion. That's an increase of more than eighty million people a year, but it's exponential. The more people there are, the more quickly it increases. We are adding almost a hundred million people a year. At this rate, in eight years, we will have hit nine billion people, a figure widely recognized as the limit of what the planet can handle.

"This has two primary consequences. The most obvious one is trash, waste. Each person on the planet today produces an average of three to three and a half pounds of waste every day. If you include bodily waste, that goes up to about five pounds. That is roughly forty billion pounds of waste every day, plus the industrial waste generated to provide food, clothing, housing, and entertainment for those people."

He gave a small snort of a laugh. "And despite that most deadly of plagues, COVID 19, the numbers keep growing." He leaned toward Gallin like they were having a fascinating conversation. "You know what I did? During lockdown, when the most densely populated, vulnerable areas of the world were completely unregulated and uncontrolled—definitely *not* locked down—everybody mixing with each other, swarming in the streets and shops with no face masks and no social distancing, you know what I did? I checked the World Population Clock on Google, every day. It did not falter for a second! *Not for a second*. And I kept asking myself and my colleagues, 'Where are all the dead? Where are the hundreds of millions who should be dying in the Third World? There should be *hundreds of millions* of dead. Where are they?"

I sighed. "Is this part of the brief you gave Geller?"

"No, Mr. Mason, but you might find it's related if you just take your blinders off for five minutes." He took a moment to gather his thoughts. "So the other effect of such a massive population is more subtle and more difficult to explain."

Gallin said, "Go ahead. We'll do our best."

He held out his right hand like he had Yorick's skull in it. "The perfect democracy is one person, right?" He closed his eyes and shook his head. "You don't need to think about it. It is self-evident. You are always the majority."

We both shrugged. It was kind of self-evident.

"However, the more people you add, the more complicated things start to get, because people start disagreeing with each other, forming pressure groups, lobbies, opposing parties. But still, if you're dealing in thousands, or even tens or hundreds of thousands, you've still got a pretty efficient democracy working. Accountability is comparatively easy to impose." He gave a sudden, unexpected laugh. "You know, in the Great Recession of the late 2000s, Iceland was the only country on the planet that sent the bankers to prison. That's an independent nation of two hundred and fifty thousand people. That's what *I* call accountability and a working democracy. The government is accountable to the people.

"But the greater the number of people, the more the individual is lost in the masses, and society begins to separate into *groups* and *categories* instead of individual human being: men and women, Black and white, gay and straight, Jewish and everybody else. Everyone wants a voice, but with so many people, it's hard to be heard unless you belong to a group that represents your category of person. Short people, tall people, fat people, thin people. And happily for our rulers, it's so much easier to manage people when you have them all divided up and categorized into groups that way. We can even invent groups to subdivide them more: Republicans, conservatives, socialists, radicals. Eventually there comes a point where you can *only* have a voice if you belong to a category. 'We speak for Blacks,' 'We speak for transsexuals,' 'The Society for Big-Eared Academics speaks for me.' And the result? Individuals become *antisocial* and must be stamped out.

"Each category is a cell that makes up the hive of society. Once you reach that stage, democracy withers and dies a natural death, along with the individual; and now one very special type of cell takes over. The cell composed of what Nietzsche and Hitler called the Supermen. Those people liberated from moral inhibitions, endowed with limitless energy who will work tirelessly to make their billions and get membership to the club. And once there, they will, from the World

Economic Forum in Cologne and the movable feast of Bilderberg, using AI, move and manipulate all those other cells to their own, ever increasing advantage." He suddenly threw back his head and laughed uproariously. "Did *you* go out and clap?" He looked from me to Gallin and back again. "Did you bleat like sheep and go and clap when they told you to? Did you applaud the organs of authority for the magnificent job they were doing, fining us for not breathing our own CO2?"

Gallin said, "What was the question the report was intended to answer?"

He held her eye. "Is there a cabal—and at that point it lists a series of names which I was not allowed to see—seeking to subject the United States of America, the European Union, and the United Kingdom of Great Britain and Northern Ireland to a dystopian, totalitarian system of government, using artificial intelligence and a militarized police force?"

Gallin ran her fingers through her hair. "Sweet Jesus!"

Glazerson nodded. "Elohim Adirim."

I sighed. "This is insane."

He looked at me through his thick lenses and said, very quietly, "People are insane, Mr. Mason. Take a passing glance at history. Look around you. Do you see a sane world? Let me ask you something. Take a longer look back through history. Has there *ever* been a sane world? Do you really think that if Caesar or Alexander had had our technology, they would not have used it?

"The world is insane, and the most insane people of all are the most powerful of all. Crazy, dangerous, violent people become powerful. And powerful people become even more dangerous and violent because they become even crazier. They think they are invincible, invulnerable. Is what your boss asked Professor Geller any crazier than the Third Reich and the death camps? Is it much crazier than the Soviet Union or the Republic of China? Is it much crazier than North Korea, Afghanistan, or Iran today? Is it crazier than shooting people in the street for singing songs at a wedding or watching TV? Or perhaps you think those things could never happen in the West."

I had no answer for him. He shrugged. "Your bosses were not suggesting that our elected *governments* were, of themselves, moving that way. The way I understood it, they wanted to know whether certain groups within what Eisenhower called the Military Industrial Complex—now called the Military Industrial Intelligence Complex—could be moving society that way. They wanted to know if that was the case."

Despite the madness of it, his words had sobered me. "What's your opinion?" I asked.

"My opinion?" He removed his glasses and wiped the lenses. As he wiped, he said, "My opinion is that you crazy bastards will all wipe each other out, and Israel will finally be left in peace to get back to the Garden." He put his glasses back on and stood. "Thank you for the coffee. I have nothing more to tell you. Unless you both plan to destroy me in the name of your democracy, Mr. Mason, I am going to leave."

"Just one more thing before you go, Professor." It was Gallin. He stopped and looked at her but said nothing. "Did Dr. Natalya Ivanova go to London for legitimate professional reasons?"

"She went for a conference and is due back in a couple of days. I'll e-mail you her address."

I said, "If Professor Geller was in fear for his life, who would he have entrusted with his research?"

"His attorney."

And with that, he turned and left.

FIVE

We touched down at London's City Airport at eight a.m. the next morning. I'd spoken to an officer from MI5 the night before, and he met us as we emerged from the private terminal. He was well dressed, in his sixties, and had the air of a man recently confined to a desk job. He provided us with a couple of files I'd asked him for and the keys to Professor Geller's apartment on Kensington Church Street. As he walked us through the jostling crowds toward the parking lot where Gallin had her car, I asked him, "What about Dr. Ivanova? Did you find her?"

"She's exactly where Glazerson said she'd be, at the Savoy. She spends most of her time in her room, with occasional walks down the road to Kings College."

"Visitors?"

"None."

We'd arrived at Gallin's TVR Cerbera and stopped. While she unlocked the car, I told him, "We'll be dropping in to see her in a couple of hours. Keep me posted if she does anything, but above all, don't let her leave. Even if it means blowing your cover. Keep her there."

He nodded. "I'll pass it on to the team watching her."

As we pulled out of the airport, it was raining. The sky was dense and gray over the gray roads, and the downpour was raising a gray mist over the blacktop. Even the red brick buildings with white stucco around Canary Warf and Limehouse and the big red buses looked gray.

We moved through Whitechapel and picked up the A40 at St Paul's Cathedral. That carried us down Oxford Street and past Hyde Park to Notting Hill Gate. Everywhere you looked, there were umbrellas tilted at a twenty-two point five degree angle with people under them also tilted at a twenty-two point five degree angle, hunched against the rain.

We ducked down Palace Gardens Terrace and into Kensington Church Street, and a minute later, she did an illegal U-turn that made a taxi slam on his breaks, honk his horn, lean out of his window, and shout things his mother would not have approved of. She pulled up outside the Newton Court apartment block and leaned out her own window as the taxi passed.

"*That's what my dad did to your wife last night, asshole! Only coz she paid him, and he put a paper nag over her head!*"

She looked at me and shrugged. "What?"

"This is what you call a low profile, Gallin?"

She grinned. "Blending in." She grabbed the files and climbed out of the car.

Inside, the lobby was carpeted in burgundy Wilton. The walls were papered in a restful sage green, and there were small, brass art deco lamps on the walls. The elevator had shiny brass concertina doors and looked like an original from the same era. It carried us smoothly to the sixth floor. The apartment was on our right, at the end of a landing with relaxing green Wilton carpets and burgundy walls with brass art deco lamps.

The door was heavy mahogany and opened onto a small entrance hall. Ahead of us, there was a full-length mirror and beside it some wooden pegs where you could hang your coat or your hat. On the other side, my left, there was a stand with a potted plant and a lamp. On the left also were double doors with small glass panels depicting stylized art deco flowers. Gallin opened them, and we went through.

It was a spacious room with two large windows over-looking Church Street, a sitting area on the right with an Arne Vodder sofa and a couple of chesterfield chairs. There was a large TV opposite the sofa and an eclectic collection of book-cases, lamp tables, lamps, and knickknacks. And books. Lots and lots of books, ranging from Rex Stout and Agatha Christie to Jared Diamond, James M. McPherson, Professor Roger Penrose, and Dale Davidson with William Rees-Mogg.

While I was looking at his books, Gallin was looking at the sofa, examining the blood spatter and the dry gore.

"He was found November 8th," she said suddenly. Her voice sounded loud in the silent apartment where death was still present in the corners and the shadows.

I glanced at her, then back at the books. "Who found him?"

She checked the file. "The cleaner. She turned up at eleven. Had her own key. Let herself in. She heard the television in the living room, which she said was unusual, but thought no more of it. She did some stuff in the kitchen and came into the living room to find Geller dead on the sofa. That was at eleven-fifteen."

I tore myself away from his books and sat in one of the chesterfields, watching Gallin. She had put the file on the coffee table and was standing about twelve feet from the sofa, staring at it. I knew she was trying to visualize what happened and get into the killer's mind.

"He was last seen Wednesday the 6th, right? At about nine-thirty or ten p.m. That's thirty-seven hours and forty-five minutes."

She was nodding but still staring at the sofa. "Time of death is basically all of Thursday, with a little bit of Wednesday evening and a little of Friday morning. He was last seen by Orlev. How does this happen?" She frowned at me. "He's sitting, looking at the TV, and he doesn't notice this person standing in the middle of the floor pull out a gun and aim it at him?"

The question was impossible to answer, so I ignored it and asked one of my own instead. "How do we know Orlev was the last person to see him?"

She went and opened the windows and looked out. She spoke absently, almost to herself.

"He flew from London to DC for a meeting with Nero. They spoke on the phone, but Orlev never showed up for the meeting." She pointed at the coffee table. "It's in the file. That's why they put Blakelock on to him."

I sighed and stood, and we did the rounds of the apartment, examining every room. I made a point of checking every window. In the last bedroom, I finally reiterated what Nero had already told us.

"The only access to the apartment is through the front

door, and there was no forced entry. As you said, Geller was sitting on his sofa facing the television. He wasn't even looking at his killer. That tells us at least one thing, and possibly two. Unless the killer was invisible, he knew his killer and had a degree of familiarity with him where he could be watching TV while they were in the room."

"We kind of knew that. What's the other thing?"

"We now also know that Geller was a misogynist and very disrespectful with women. That attitude of sitting watching TV while somebody is standing in the middle of the room, it is not hard to visualize that as a disrespectful gesture toward a woman. Am I wrong?"

She shook her head. "No, you're not wrong."

"And if that were correct, we could be looking at one of three people."

"A prostitute, Dr. Natalya Ivanova, or his wife."

"Right. Now, baby steps: if it was an escort, or some kind of sex worker—"

"Are you turning woke on me?"

"Shut up. If she was a prostitute, it means that somehow, whoever wanted him dead had managed to plant her." She thought about it. "That would not be easy to do. That would take a lot of setting up."

I nodded. "I agree. So—"

"So unless it was his wife, we would be looking at a honey trap."

"Right, and that puts Natalya Ivanova squarely in the frame."

She sighed. "I don't know, Mason. A beautiful Russian academic who is also a trained killer working for the Military Industrial Intelligence Complex? Even in the kind of crazy world Glazerson was talking about, that's a bit rich. Also, and allowing for the fact that the Russians are about as subtle as a luminous, inflatable condom, if she was planning to kill Geller, would she *really* tell his wife she was coming out to see him?"

We fell silent for a moment. Then, as she so often did, she spoke my thoughts. "But on the other hand, Mason, who says she did? We only have her word for it that meeting in the store ever happened. Think about it. If Mrs. Geller had flown to London for the express purpose of killing her husband, it would be very subtle and very smart indeed to tell us Dr. Ivanova was coming to see him."

I nodded. For some reason, it made more sense now than when she'd first floated the idea back in Tel Aviv. "So the meeting at the store might never have happened. She heard through an acquaintance, whoever, that Ivanova was going to London. In her mind, she drew her own conclusions. It is, as you said, the straw that broke the camel's back. She came to confront him. He ignored her, switched on the TV in his inimitable style, she pulled the gun, and bam!"

She sighed again. "It has the ring of truth, but there are irritating little details."

"Like how did she get the gun into the country. The UK is very strict on that score. If she didn't bring it with her, where the hell does Mrs. Geller get a 9 mm semi-automatic in London? Also, Orlev..."

She nodded ponderously. "Orlev, the last person to see him alive, winds up with all the research they have done on a flash drive. Where is the rest of it? Where are the laptops, the hard drives, the notebooks? Where has it all gone, and why does Orlev have pretty much all of it on one flash drive?"

I said, "Exactly," then shrugged and spread my hands.

"Nero told us: because Geller suspected someone was going to kill him he made the drive and gave it to Orlev. But that in itself seriously weakens the Mrs. Geller hypothesis."

She gently, absently punched the wall, turned, and walked back to the living room. I followed her, and she sat on the chesterfield I had just vacated. I stood in the middle of the floor, watching her. She ran her fingers through her hair and leaned back.

"So if we follow that route, what are we saying? Orlev has come to realize the importance and the value of the report. He realizes there are people in the Military Industrial Intelligence Complex who will pay a lot of money for that report. Geller tells him he fears for his life and has prepared the flash drive for him. So Orlev comes over to London and shoots Geller in the head. Then takes all the notebooks, laptops et cetera and dumps them off a cliff in Cornwall. He then flies back to Washington."

I paused, and she said, "And that's where it starts to come apart. Why does he go crazy when he hears the news that Geller is dead? He *knows* he's dead because *he* killed him. If he's done this, why go to DC at all? Why not call whoever he's going to sell this stuff to and meet them out in Menorca? Or some place else? His behavior after the killing does not make sense if he is the killer. And what about the stuff Blakelock found in the pool? He didn't chuck that off a cliff in Cornwall."

I paced the room for a bit, then stopped, looking at the floor and scratching my head.

"Orlev told Nero that about a week before Geller was killed he called him and told him he thought somebody wanted to kill him, right?" I wagged a finger at her. "It was after that he gave Orlev the flash drive, and remember, he said he himself had voluntarily destroyed everything else. Yasha Orlev contacted Nero with this information just under two days before Geller's murder, which puts it at precisely the last time Geller was seen alive—by Orlev." I wagged a finger at her again. "Remember this guy is a little crazy and very smart. So what if he decides to play it out? He goes to DC, knowing he is going to receive the news of his pal's death when he gets there. And when he gets the news, he plays the part and goes off the rails, as you'd expect him to. Then vanishes. He goes to his little fortress in Menorca, where he has arranged to meet his buyer. But the buyer has no interest in buying what he can get for free with a little persuasion. He tortures Orlev and kills him."

She took over. "And right then Blakelock shows up. He nails the killer, recovers the drive and..." She trailed off and spread her hands.

I shrugged. "And either Blakelock has the drive and is selling it to the highest bidder, or Blakelock is dead and the Military Industrial Intelligence Complex—from here on in MIC—have it securely in their possession." I sighed as I watched her shake her head. "The pieces fit, more or less, but it doesn't ring true."

"I agree." She shrugged. "Why *bother* going back to DC? What did he stand to gain by doing that? And why would MIC bother to torture and kill him if he was willingly handing over the goods? Just to save money? I don't think so. No, there's something we are missing, Mason. There is a dimension to this we are not getting."

I pointed at her and wagged my finger. "And the reason is, we don't know who the hell we are chasing. We are searching a haystack, and we don't even know if we're looking for a needle or…" I waved my hands helplessly. "Either way we need to either confirm or eliminate Dr. Ivanova. We need to do that and see if she confirms Mrs. Geller's story about meeting in the store."

She nodded. "Yeah, c'mon. Let's go."

We stepped out onto the landing, and the door opposite opened. A man in his early forties emerged and frowned at us.

"Who are you?" he said.

I was about to ask him the same question, but Gallin said, "MI5" and showed him her card. He took her card and stared at it, frowning. "*MI5?* What on earth is going on here? It's been bedlam for the last few days. Now MI5?"

"Did you know Professor Geller?"

"We'd met a couple of times in the lift. He seemed harmless enough. Now I hear he's been murdered!"

"I'm Captain Aila Gallin, this is my colleague Alex Mason."

"Nick Barns."

We shook, and Gallin went on. "Were you here on the night of the 7th November?"

"Yes, we were at home all evening. In fact, we are here most of the time. I'm one of the many casualties of COVID, and I work from home. So does my wife. We take it in turns to make the school trip."

"Do you mind me asking, who is 'we'?"

"Myself, my wife Jody, and our daughter Jane."

Gallin glanced a frown at me, then asked Barns, "Have the police not taken statements from you?"

He shrugged. "We offered, but as the constable was sitting down to take them, he was called away, and the inspector said somebody would be around to see us. I thought it might be you."

I said, "So either you or your wife, or all three of you were home from the night of the 6th through to the morning of the 8th."

He nodded once. "And we didn't hear an altercation or a shot or anything."

Gallin smiled. "A pistol shot sounds very much like a firecracker. They don't sound the way they do in the movies."

"I know what a gun sounds like, Captain Gallin. No, we didn't hear a thing. Obviously there was his friend who stays sometimes. He left on the Wednesday evening. Then he had a visitor on Thursday afternoon—"

"A visitor?"

"Well, we heard voices on the landing. One doesn't want to pry—"

Gallin said, "Male or female?"

"Hard to tell, could have been either really."

A woman peered around the door behind him and said softly, "I think it was a woman."

Gallin asked, "Are you Mrs. Barns?"

"Yes."

"Did you hear them talking?"

"Briefly, when she was leaving."

"So when she left, she was talking to him?"

"That was the impression I got. They spoke softly. He had seen her to the door, and they were saying good bye."

"Will you be in this evening?"

"Yes, of course."

"I'm going to send someone to get a full statement from

you." She smiled and held out her hand. "You have been extremely helpful. Thank you so much."

In the elevator on the way down, she arched an eyebrow at me.

"You were going to ask him who the hell he was and give him a hard time, weren't you?"

I didn't answer.

SIX

Outside there was a steady hiss from the wet roads. Big red busses and big black taxi cabs cast red and green light on wet blacktop, and shop fronts cast an amber glow on the sidewalks. Overhead, bloated clouds sagged dark and heavy. I smelled the damp air and quoted that poem by Thomas Hood.

"No warmth, no cheerfulness, no healthy ease, No comfortable feel in any member, No shade, no shine, no butterflies no bees, No fruits, no flowers, no leaves, no birds! November!"

She gave a rueful smile on one side of her face and climbed behind the wheel of her monster car. I got in the other side, and she rubbed her hands. I spoke before she could draw breath.

"We need to pause. I, at least, need to pause. The last person to see Professor David Geller alive was a woman who showed up Thursday afternoon."

She fired up the big brute, and the engine growled. But she

didn't pull away. She dropped her hands in her lap and said, "No shots were fired, and he was apparently alive when she left, because he was at the door, seeing her off."

I grunted. "No shots were heard."

She sighed, pulled out, and did another U-turn into the traffic, peering into her wing mirror.

"Mason, you know what I am thinking?"

"Probably not."

"The Barns family are there all day, right?"

"Right."

"Nobody heard a shot, from Wednesday to Friday. So as you insinuated, maybe he used a suppressor. But we also have the fact that the lock was not picked. So either Geller let his killer in, or the killer had a key."

"You're back to Orlev. I said I needed to pause."

"Hear me out. How does this pan? The killer shows up at two or three in the morning, when the Barnses are all asleep. For some reason, he has a key and lets himself in. He expects Geller to be asleep but finds him watching TV. Nothing unusual in that for a restless genius. He shoots him, and the Barns family don't hear because they are in their bedrooms fast asleep."

"This is how you pause?"

"We haven't got time to pause, Mason."

"We haven't got time to get it wrong, either."

"Pause after we talk to Dr. Natalya Ivanova. She's at the Savoy." She glanced at me. "I want her out of your mind. I told you, the only place you're going to find a beautiful Russian spy called Dr. Natalya Ivanova, who is also an ice-cold assassin who kills an Israeli professor working for the Mossad is in Ian Fleming's fevered imagination."

We turned east onto Kensington High Street and cruised through the drizzle toward Knightsbridge.

By the time we pulled into the Savoy, the heavy clouds and the short winter days had conspired and, though it was barely three p.m., it was already getting dark. My stomach complained that it felt like dinner time and we hadn't even had lunch yet. I told it to blame Gallin, who was being particularly obnoxious at the moment. It replied I should cowboy up and be a man.

All of that got us as far as Dr. Ivanova's door. I knocked, and she opened and frowned at us. I frowned too. She was not what I had expected. She was the girl next door, only with something added that was hard to define.

"Dr. Ivanova?"

"Yes, who are you?"

"My name is Alex Mason. I work for the Department of Intelligence at the Pentagon. This is my colleague, Captain Aila Gallin. She works for MI5. May we come in?"

"Is this about Poor David—Professor Geller?"

"Yes."

She stepped back to let us in, and I was surprised to see that what she had was a suite. I somehow doubted the University of Tel Aviv ran to suites at the Savoy for its lecturers. She showed us into her sitting room and ushered us to a sofa and a couple of chairs.

"Please," she said and sat. I studied her a moment and saw that her cheeks were flushed pink and her blue eyes were bright. I decided she was worried, maybe even scared.

Gallin leaned forward with her elbows on her knees and spoke softly. "We won't take up a lot of your time, Dr. Ivanova. We just have a couple of questions. They are rather sensitive, but I hope you will appreciate the need to be absolutely honest." She gave that woman-of-the-world smile and added, "I also want to stress to you that we are not the police. It is in our power to be a lot more discreet than the police."

Dr. Ivanova's cheeks had gone from pink to almost red. "Perhaps you had better ask your questions, Captain Gallin."

"Did you bump into Mrs. Geller a couple of days before you flew to London from Tel Aviv?"

She frowned like it was the weirdest question she had ever been asked. She glanced at me, then back at Gallin. "Marian? No, I haven't seen Marian for weeks, perhaps a couple of months. Why?"

"Were you and Professor Geller having an affair, Dr. Ivanova?"

"How dare you—"

I cut in. "This is a murder inquiry, Dr. Ivanova, and as you are already aware, it has elements of international espionage at the highest level. So we dare, and you would be very well advised to cooperate with us fully. Now, again, were you sexually or romantically involved with Professor Geller?"

She gave me that look women give you when they figure you just proved that all men are bastards. She closed her eyes and took a deep breath, but her cheeks didn't stop burning.

"Very briefly, David and I had an—we had a *relationship*." She opened her eyes and turned to Gallin. Maybe she thought Gallin would be more sympathetic. "David was a very hard man to resist. He was extremely intense. Uncompromising. And"—she shook her head like she didn't believe her own words—"*completely* amoral! The things he did, his ethics, they had nothing to do with what was right or wrong. All that mattered was what he wanted."

I saw Gallin's eyebrows rise, but I wasn't surprised at what

Dr. Ivanova had said. I had already reached that conclusion about him. I knew the type.

"Did he talk to you about his research, what he was doing here in London?"

"No!" She looked shocked and gave a laugh like I was nuts. "There were three things of maximum importance in David's life. In reverse order, they were sex, his work, and Israel. I never met a man who was more insanely nationalistic and patriotic."

I arched an eyebrow. "What has his patriotism got to do with his research, Dr. Ivanova?"

"Oh, don't worry, Mr. Mason. He told me, and every other woman he wanted to have sex with, that the government gave him top clearance and commissioned him work of national security status. Everything and anything to give him glamor and sex appeal. But never a word about the work itself."

"You admired him?"

"Yes, very much. He was crazy. The world was too small for him. He said, 'Every Jew must be David and kill the Nephilim!'"

Gallin frowned. "What did he mean by that?"

"He had a crazy 'theory.'" She made inverted commas with her fingers. "It was not really a theory but a crazy idea. He told me once when he was drunk. He thought the world was run by fallen angels, the Nephilim, and it was the destiny of Israel, the chosen people, to stand against them. Always! He was constantly repeating, 'The name of God is Ehye asher Ehye! I am that I am! This is our god! Let the Nephilim tremble!' Crazy, but he was also fascinating and brilliant, and I did admire him."

Gallin said, "Your purpose for coming to London..."

Dr. Ivanova smiled and shook her head. She seemed to be

relaxing, as though our knowing about her affair had set her at ease.

"No, Captain Gallin. That was a happy coincidence, nothing more."

"When was the last time you saw Professor Geller?"

She became abstracted and turned her gaze toward the gray window. "Thursday," she said, "the day before he was murdered."

I asked, "Where was that? Where did you meet?"

"I went to see him at his apartment. I..."

She faltered. I spoke softly. "What, Dr. Ivanova? What was the purpose of your visit?"

"We had started our affair in Tel Aviv. I couldn't resist him, but I felt bad about his wife. She is a beautiful woman but small, ineffectual, weak. But she is also kind and good, and I hated the way he treated her."

Gallin said, "Wasn't that how he treated all women? Didn't he treat you like that too?"

"Ha!" Her eyes were bright, and there was arrogance and defiance in that single laugh. "He tried, but no man treats me like that! And I let him know it!"

"So," I said, easing her back on track, "the purpose of your visit?"

"I told you it was a short relationship. It was never going to be anything else. My fascination was satisfied, and his work and his country were always going to take precedence over me. So I went to tell him we were finished. I was going soon back to Tel Aviv, he was staying in London for the immediate future, and he was married to a lovely woman. We were done."

It sounded rehearsed, but it also sounded believable. I

could see the scene playing itself out in my mind. I asked her, "How did he take that?"

Her cheeks colored again, and her jaw clenched. "Typical David. He switches on the television and tells me, 'Yeah, OK. Call me when your menstruation is finished. You know where the door is.'"

There was a heavy silence. She closed her eyes and bit her lip. After a moment, she shrugged.

"Before, I would have gotten mad at him and shouted, and we would have had a fight, and then after the fight make up, da, da, da..." She made an on-and-on gesture with her hand. "But not this time. I told him, 'David, I am leaving. Please at least show me to the door.' He made a big show of huffing and puffing, and at the door he asks me, 'Will I see you in Tel Aviv?' I told him no. And that was the last time I saw him."

Gallin asked her, "How did you find out he had been killed?"

"Professor Glazerson telephoned and told me." She seemed to shudder, and her cheeks went pasty. "I keep thinking that while I was there, talking to him, perhaps there was somebody outside waiting for me to leave. But why would anybody want to kill David? He was eccentric, crazy, but he hurt nobody..." She paused and trailed off. "Well, he hurt nobody except his wife."

I arched an ironic eyebrow at her. "Maybe it was the Nephilim." Her face told me she didn't think I was awful funny. I ignored it and plowed on. "Dr. Ivanova, forgive me, but I think you are lying."

Her eyes went wide. "I am *not* lying!"

I gestured at her with my open hand. "I am sitting here, looking at you, and I do not see a woman who casually slips into an affair with a married man and after a few encounters finds she is sexually satiated and calls it a day. What I see is a highly intelligent, very attractive woman who has fulfilled her ambitions and could, frankly, have her pick of men who could satisfy her intellectually, emotionally, and physically."

She sat blinking at me with her eyebrows close to her hairline. I gave it a moment to sink in, and then drove it home. "I think you were in love with Dr. Geller because you had never met a man like him."

She didn't answer, which was as good as an affirmative. She looked away, back at the gray window, and her beautiful face seemed to age and sag.

"You are a big bastard, eh, Mr. Mason?"

"We need to get at the truth, Dr. Ivanova, and it won't help if you lie to us just to protect your vanity."

"Yes!" She scowled at me. "I was in love with David. But he was not in love with me. He was in love only with himself and Israel! In the short time we were together, I neglected my work, tried to support *him* in *his* work. His work seemed so much more important than mine. He made it seem everything in the world depended on his work."

I asked gently, "How did you support him in his work if he didn't tell you about it?"

"No, no." She shook her head. "Don't try to trap me, Mr. Mason. I stroked his hair and kissed his face while he was reading or typing. I made him coffee just how he liked it, not instant like his wife makes it. I cooked for him, massage... Anything, everything, I was there for him."

"You wanted to move in together."

She nodded. "I told him, 'Divorce your wife. I am a better woman for you.'"

"And he said no."

"The bastard said no. He wanted to stay with his wife."

"That's what you talked about when you went to see him on Thursday."

She nodded and sobbed suddenly, just once. "That is what I went to see him about on Thursday."

Gallin sighed and shook her head. "You realize, Dr. Ivanova, that this gives you a powerful motive for killing him."

"No." She shook her head. "I might claw his eyes out. I might stick a knife in him. But I cannot use a gun. I cannot shoot someone. To kill for love is a passionate thing. A gun is a cold weapon, distant. A firearm, yes, but it should be called an ice weapon. So cold." She held out both arms in front of her. "Bang, all finished."

"Son of a bitch." It was Gallin. "I wouldn't have blamed you." She showed me a defiant face. "What? I'm not a cop. I can say things like that. He was a misogynistic bastard going through life exploiting the women he came across."

I frowned. "Dial it down, Gallin, will you?"

She ignored me and turned back to Ivanova. "Was there anything he said, anything at all that he told you that might give you some idea of who was waiting outside...?"

"I don't know that anyone was waiting outside. I just got that feeling sometimes, like a creeping fear. What if I had been there when they arrived?"

"But you have no idea who 'they' might be?"

"No, I'm sorry. I'm afraid not. He let me make coffee for him, but he never talked to me about his research."

I said, "Dr. Ivanova, I have just a couple more questions and then I think for now we're done."

"For now?"

"Yeah, for now. Are you Jewish?"

She stared at me fixedly for a moment. "Does that make a difference?"

"I don't know. Does it?"

"I am of Russian Jewish descent, Mr. Mason, yes."

"So that was a passion you shared."

She didn't answer right away but then said, "Yes."

"And one last thing. Who was Professor Geller's attorney here in London?"

"I have no idea."

"He never talked about his attorney?"

"No, never."

I looked at Gallin. "You have any more questions?"

She shook her head. "I'm good."

I stood. "I am sorry to have intruded upon your grief." I handed her my card. "Finding out who killed Professor Geller, and why he was killed, is extremely important, Dr. Ivanova. More than you might think. If anything comes to mind, anything at all, however trivial, please let us know."

SEVEN

GALLIN FOLLOWED THE STRAND AND THE MALL through the rain as far as Hyde Park. There she turned north. She followed Church Street up to Notting Hill Gate and there turned down into Portobello Road. All the way she was silent. The only sound was the growl of the TVR's brutal engine and the rhythmic squeak of wipers on the windshield.

Roads in London are not like roads in the States. There is no grid system. These are roads that might have started as beaten paths for hunter gatherers back in the Ice Age. As societies were born and grew, buildings gradually appeared along their edges. Inns and shops became villages, and the tracks became roads and highways and eventually acquired names like Wine Office Court, Shoe Lane, and Mason Cutter Street. They wind and twist with no apparent logic among elegant Georgian and Edwardian houses, among a superabundance of plane trees, gardens, and parks, and if you are able to find an actual, real Londoner today, he will tell you that any road that is straight for more than a mile was probably made by the Romans.

Portobello is not a Roman road, and as we crawled along it, among the hiss and the splash of the evening rain with the light from the shop fronts spilling onto the wet sidewalks, it dawned on me that I was in the heart of one of the largest cities on the planet, but the road I was on could be in a small town anywhere in the UK, New England, or the Midwest. And something Nero had once said to me flashed into my mind.

"It was in those small villages in northwest Europe," he had said, "that true democracy was born. Not in the Greek agoras, but among the thatched cottages of Britain and Scandinavia."

We eventually pulled up outside a café-cum-restaurant opposite a Spanish grocery store. We climbed out, hunched into our shoulders, and crossed the sidewalk under the awning. A bell clanged as we went in to the warmth inside. It smelled good, of frying green peppers and onions and meat. Only a couple of tables were occupied, and there was a low murmur of conversation.

A waitress with a nice smile and enough pins in her to start a tailoring business greeted Gallin like she knew her and led us to a table in a dark corner. Outside there was a roll of thunder, and for a moment the lights flickered. Somewhere a woman gave a startled "Oh!" and people laughed.

We sat. Gallin told the girl, "Bring me two large Bushmills, and open a bottle of Rioja. If it's alive, it needs to breathe."

She took the menus from the girl's hand and gave me one of them.

"OK." I said it with a hint of irony.

She glanced at me like she was going to throw the table at me. "What?"

"I think it's a good idea," I told the menu. "Let's go somewhere, have a drink and an early supper and discuss this whole thing. See if we can get some kind of a handle on it."

"What?" she said again, suppressing a smile. "Suddenly you can't read my mind?"

The drinks came, and Gallin ordered some kind of weird fusion thing that involved noodles, rice, organic meat in a tomato sauce, ginger, brown muscovado sugar, and soy sauce. There might have been some chocolate and chili in there too.

The waitress brought our whiskeys, and Gallin took them and asked me, "You want to tell me what you're thinking?" She said it, leaned forward with her elbows on the table, and put her hands together in front of her face like she was praying. I knew what was coming next. "I'll tell you what *I* think."

"Go on." I sipped my whiskey.

"We are going crazy—"

"That would explain a few things."

She blinked but didn't smile. "We are going crazy because we have two alternative approaches, and we are saying, 'It's got to be one or the other. It has to be this way, or it has to be that way.'" She sat back and wagged a finger at me. "But actually, what has happened is that it's both."

"You need to explain that."

"We have two alternative possibilities—what you Americans would call alternate possibilities." She paused and narrowed her eyes. "Which just means that one possibility comes after the other."

"I am looking forward to your mood improving, Gallin. You want to take a shot of whiskey and get back on track?"

"Fine." She took a pull and smacked her lips. "So we have two *alternative* possibilities. One: Geller, and then Orlev, were murdered for the research they had done and the report they had written. Two: Geller was murdered by a jealous woman, and we don't know exactly why Orlev was murdered. Neither of these two is really satisfactory. But what if—" She sagged a moment and leaned forward into her praying position again. "You know, Mason, life isn't all just about one thing or another. That was partly Geller's problem, right? He was focused on three things and didn't give a damn about the rest of life. But *everything* is happening! All at the same time. And sometimes, often, things overlap, collide, get mixed up." We stared at each other a moment. Then she erupted again, "A person is doing a job, she is focused on that job, it's all of her life, and suddenly this guy comes along, and her focus is suddenly all over the place because he has stimulated feelings in her and, from the inside, from *her* perspective, her behavior is coherent, but from the outside, from other people's perspective, it looks completely *in*coherent."

I was frowning hard, feeling distracted and incoherent. All I said was, "OK..."

"So what I am saying is that two motives, from two totally unrelated people, might have overlapped, and we would be remiss to focus on only one."

I nodded, spread my hands, and shrugged. "Sure, but we still have the same problem. Ivanova has all the motivation she might need to kill him. Just like Mrs. Geller has. And there are probably a few more women out there who had motive. Geller seems to have been a guy who knew how to make women want to kill him. But it's the killing itself. I don't see passion or hatred in the killing. Ivanova said it herself. It was cold and clinical."

She shook her head. "I don't know, Mason, when she

described that scene, where she was leaving, and he switched on the TV and said, 'Let me know when your menstruation is finished.' I just remembered what you said, about the straw that broke the camel's back."

"I was quoting you. I was talking about Mrs. Geller, and I have to say I am beginning to agree with you. A beautiful Russian academic who is also an ice-cold killer?" I shook my head. "You asked me what I think. I think we have two assassinations on our hands. These are not murders, they are assassinations. And there is a key point we have been ignoring."

She scowled. "What?"

"The very significant fact that Orlev was tortured but Geller wasn't."

"Shit."

"It tells us a lot about the motive behind each killing. My reading is that Geller was killed to silence him. Orlev was killed while trying to recover the drive. And *that* suggests strongly to me that they were sequential and related."

She took a deep breath, held it, and spread her hands. "If that is right then what we are saying is that we have—or had—a professional assassin on our hands in the pay of some organization within the Military Industrial Intelligence Complex."

I shrugged. "It's what Nero implied and what's been staring us in the face from the beginning, but we got sidetracked by the women."

"Story of your life, huh?"

"What life?" I said with more bitterness than I had intended. "The only distraction I get these days is from Manny Pacquiao."

"Stop, you're breaking my heart."

I snorted. "What heart?"

The food arrived along with the bottle of Rioja, and we ate in silence for a while. Eventually she sat back, chewing, and spoke with her mouth full. "If you're right, which for once you probably are, our suspect is dead in Menorca, where Peter Blakelock killed him. But then we have to ask two questions: one, why didn't the Barnses hear the killer arrive and leave when they seem to have heard everybody else? And two, what happened to Peter Blakelock? Maybe one person we should be looking at is Orlev. But Orlev was Geller's best friend. They'd known each other for years and often worked together. It is unlikely he would suddenly turn like that." She raised both hands to ward off my reply. "But allowing for a moment that MIC had got to him through bribes, threats or both, it makes no sense that they would then torture him."

I broke a piece of bread and mopped sauce while I thought. "Geller said he was scared he was being followed and thought he might be in danger, right?"

"Yes, that's true."

"So follow me. Exactly as he told Nero, he destroys everything after putting it on that drive. Somehow this MIC hit man finds out what has happened, but he's too late. So he kills Geller and goes after Orlev."

She sighed and ate. "A hit man who works for the Military Industrial Intelligence Complex, who is either invisible or was a close friend of Geller's."

"If they work for the Military Industrial Intelligence Complex, they are the best of the best. They've been trained by Delta, the SAS, the Mossad..."

She shook her head. "I've spent my whole career up against the best. So have you. We *are* the best, Mason. And you know as well as I do that when they have been at the scene, when they have done a job, you can *smell* them. There is something missing here, Mason. I'm telling you. We are chasing a ghost."

I studied her a moment. "A ghost?"

She nodded. "He's *invisible!* He doesn't even leave a smell."

I shook my head. "He left something; we just can't see it yet."

She made the face of depressed frustration. "And if we follow the money? Or if not the money, the benefit. Who benefits from his death?"

She had seen the absurdity of the question before she'd finished it. We exchanged ironic smiles. I said, "Grumman, Sikorsky, Lockheed, McDonald Douglas, Rolls Royce, The Federal Reserve, Microsoft, Meta... The list goes on and on. Hell, even the British Royal Family benefits. One percent of eight billion people benefit."

"Right, if what Nero says is true, the whole damned ruling elite benefits."

I shook my head. "But, Gallin, I am not willing to believe that everyone in that complex—I mean, we are talking about thousands of people, maybe tens of thousands... And I know a lot of them, most of them, are good patriots."

"No." She shook her head. "I agree. What Nero spoke about was a cabal."

"That's right." I thought about it for a moment, tipping my glass back and forth. "The thing with a cabal is that it can be very powerful in some respects but vulnerable in others. Cabals are creatures of the dark. They don't like the light. That's why they're secret. Because if they are exposed in the light, they disintegrate. They fall apart. We need something, a piece of forensic evidence, a witness, *something* that will shed some light on the cabal. Otherwise we are groping in the dark with little more than conspiracy theories."

"Sure, but like you said before, the killer is a pro that has left no evidence, and the instigator has total deniability. We are stumped."

I drained my glass, called the waitress and asked for two espressos and two double Bushmills. When she'd gone, I said, "Maybe not. Gallin, we have been neglecting the obvious."

She arched an eyebrow. "Really? There is something in this unholy mess that is obvious?"

I sucked my teeth for a minute and said, "Maybe. What do we keep getting told? That this report on this drive is of seismic importance. The commissioning of this research is no less than a declaration of war by..."—I paused, searching my mind for the right words—"an *alliance* of certain factions—perhaps elements would be a better word—of Western, democratic governments, along with Israel, against this Military Industrial Intelligence Complex, that has, by stealth, since 1947, effectively become a totalitarian government within our democracies."

She shrugged with her shoulder and with her eyebrows. "Nicely put, but we knew that."

"OK, let me finish. Now with that in mind, if this is a war, Geller and Orlev have been engaged..." I spread my hands. "They've been engaged in the Manhattan project, and they have created the atom bomb."

She smiled and gave a small laugh. "OK."

"That's what we've been told, right? This is seismic, and released by the right people it could be as far reaching as the English Reformation or the American Declaration of Independence. Am I right?"

"Right. You're right." She said it like she was biting back the need to say, "So what?"

"And that nuclear device they have created is a stick, one and a half inches long by an eighth of an inch thick and half an inch wide."

"This is fascinating, Mason, but what's your point? I don't see anything we are overlooking."

"So Geller passes the drive to Orlev, who makes a run for touch. But when he finds out Geller is dead, he loses it and runs for Menorca."

"We know this, Mason—"

I raised a finger. "Now! Nero, whom I have never known to make a foolish mistake, does...what?" She blinked a couple of times and shifted her gaze to the ceiling. I added, "Think of it *in the context of the Manhattan project*. What does he do?"

"He sends Peter Blakelock after him, to watch him."

"And what does Peter do?"

"He follows him to Menorca, kills Orlev's killer, and recovers the drive." She gave a small sarcastic laugh. "We're running around like headless chickens wondering if Marian Geller or Natalya Ivanova killed Geller, when our prime suspect is staring us in the face. Is it the guy Blakelock killed in Menorca? Is that the big revelation?"

"But, Gallin, what did Peter do then?"

She stared at me for a long moment. "He disappeared." She frowned. "He was a good man, presumed dead. Murdered."

I shook my head. "I don't know, Gallin. Expert assassins are a rare breed, and they tend to work alone. Are we saying they had *two* on Menorca to take care of Orlev, a man who was about as dangerous as lying motionless in bed?"

"That's a weird metaphor, Mason."

"That's because it's a simile, not a metaphor."

"And you're a—"

"The point is, however powerful this cabal is, they are very unlikely to send two world-class assassins to Menorca to kill a dissipated, sex-crazed academic. And if they had, they would both have been at the house, not one at the house and the other in Mahon. So that raises the question, what happened to Peter Blakelock, the last man known to have the drive?" I shook my head. "We have been remiss, Gallin. We have been wasting time looking in the wrong places."

"So you think Blakelock absconded with the drive? You think he is trying to sell it?"

I shrugged. "It would surprise me in Peter. He's a good man, and Nero trusted him. But you never can tell." I shrugged. "It's possible he has gone to ground and he is waiting for the penny to drop and someone to go and look for him. Either way, at this stage, all we can do is guess. I can't help feeling we've wasted a lot of time focusing on Geller because he was the prime target, when Orlev and Peter Blakelock were where we should have been directing our attention."

The waitress brought our coffee and whiskey. When she'd gone, Gallin picked up her glass and said, "So we're going to Menorca."

"We're going to Menorca." I raised my glass. "Cheers!"

EIGHT

THE CALL CAME WHEN WE WERE AT GALLIN'S HOUSE on Campden Hill Square, packing for the trip to Menorca. Gallin was in her room, and I was in the guest room. I put the phone to my ear and tried to fold my shirt with just my left hand.

"Hello?"

"Mr. Mason—Alex—may I call you Alex? This is Dr. Ivanova, Natalya."

I leaned out the bedroom door and spoke loudly. "Good evening, Dr. Ivanova. How can I help you?"

"I am leaving very soon, going back to Israel."

I abandoned my attempt to fold my shirt left-handed and frowned at the black glass in the window, where my ghost was frowning back at me.

"Yes," I said, "you said. In the next couple of days."

"No, Alex, sooner than that. Professor Glazerson has telephoned to me. He wants me to return immediately. I think they suspect I have killed David. I think they will interrogate me, maybe put me in prison. Maybe kill me."

I stepped over to the window and looked out at the light from the kitchen below reflecting on the sodden bog that had been Gallin's back yard.

"What makes you think that, Dr. Ivanova?"

"Please, call me Natalya." She paused like she was waiting for me to call her Natalya. I didn't, so she said, "You suspected that I killed him."

"Suspect is putting it a bit strong. It was one of a number of possibilities we were—"

"But I loved him."

I suppressed a sigh. "Dr. Ivanova, Natalya, I am not sure what—"

"Will you come and talk to me? I am so afraid. Maybe if I talk to you, you can talk to them, make them see I loved David. I would never hurt him."

"I have to catch a plane, Natalya. I am pretty sure you are not a prime suspect—"

"I can tell you things..."

In the glass in the window, I saw Gallin's reflection appear in the doorway behind me and lean against the jamb. I turned and looked at her. "What things?" I said. "We spoke just a few hours ago. What's changed?"

"I didn't tell you everything."

"Why not?"

"That is not important now. I did not like the woman, Captain Gallin. She is dangerous. She is a killer. I can see it in her eyes. I must talk to you."

"I told you I have to catch a plane. Can't you tell me now, over the phone?"

"You are not listening to me. I am going back to Israel. I might be imprisoned or killed. I may never see you again. There are things I must tell you. Delay your flight. Come and see me."

I held Gallin's eye. She was frowning. I said into the phone, "Where are you, still at the Savoy?"

"No. I made myself unrecognizable, and I have caught a bus and then the underground. Then I caught a taxi. Now I am at Daphne's, on Draycott Avenue. We can have a late supper. Do not bring your captain."

"Ok, I'll be there in half an hour."

I hung up, and Gallin said, "You'll be where in half an hour? In half an hour we'll be on our way to the airport."

"Dr. Ivanova. She says she's been called back to Israel. She's afraid they suspect her of Geller's death and they're going to arrest her and put her in prison or even kill her. She says she has information for me she wants to give me before she goes."

"Why didn't she tell you when we were there?"

"She doesn't trust you. She says you have the eyes of a killer."

She didn't answer straight away. Then she said, "And you haven't? You be careful. I don't like that woman. Will you be back tonight?"

"Of course."

"Make sure you are or I'll have to go looking for you."

I sighed and shook my head. "My mother said that to me once when I was sixteen. I didn't show up for a week." She arched a devastating eyebrow at me as I pulled on my jacket. I told her, "Come on, give me some credit. Pack a cute dress. I'll take you somewhere nice when we get to Mahon."

As I reached the bottom of the stairs, she called after me, "Mason!"

I stopped and looked back. "What?"

"You're an asshole. Be careful."

I JOINED Dr. Natalya Ivanova at a table in a corner beside an open fire. She looked beautiful, but her eyes were a little puffy and her nose was a little red, like she'd developed a cold since we'd seen her a couple of hours earlier. She was nursing a gin and tonic and watched me arrive without saying anything until I'd pulled out the chair and sat down opposite her. Then she said, "Thank you for coming."

I smiled. "I already had dinner, but you made it sound urgent."

Tears welled in her eyes, and she dabbed at them with her napkin. "Keep me company, please, Alex. I am frightened."

A waiter came with a menu. I told him to bring me a martini. Natalya gave him her order, and I told him I just wanted a sirloin steak, medium rare. When he'd left, I said, "Time to level with me, Natalya. I can only help you if you come clean. I can't do anything for you if you lie to me."

"I don't trust your Captain Gallin. She is from the Mossad, and they suspect me. They think I killed David."

"Did you?"

"I told you already, no."

"Then you have nothing to worry about."

She sneered a laugh that for a moment turned her beautiful face unattractive. "If they decide I have done it, then I am finished, whatever proof I give them."

"I think they are more interested in finding the truth than in hunting down beautiful Russian academics." That made her smile. I added, "You said you had something to tell me."

"They will kill me if I tell you."

I sighed and felt suddenly tired. I thought of Gallin back at the house, finishing her packing, or by now probably cooking a meal in the kitchen. I was tempted to stand and leave. Instead I said, "Natalya, you are an intelligent woman. Let's try to have an intelligent conversation. You already believe they are going to kill you. So unless they can kill you twice, telling me won't make any difference, will it? I can talk to the office back home, and we can probably arrange a change of identity, protection, immunity—whatever is needed. But they—and I—will want something in return, and that something is information. So let's cut the irrational, scared female act and get down to brass tacks."

She stared at me for a moment. "You are so hard. Like a brute with no feelings."

Somehow she didn't make it sound like an insult or a complaint. I said, "Are we done? You have two minutes and then I am out of here."

"No." She shook her head. "Please don't go. Stay. I will tell you."

The waiter brought my drink, poured it at the table, and left. I sipped it and asked her, "Tell me what?"

"David and I were close, more close than I made you think."

"How close?"

"He fascinated me. He was a small man, not a physical animal like you, but in his mind and his personality, he was a giant, ruthless, a monster." I waited, watching her. "And for him, I was something he said he had never found before, a woman who was beautiful and sexual but also intelligent, able to think, explore, and analyze like a man. He adored me. He said that I was his goddess and I helped him to escape from the prison of his intellect."

"Fascinating. I get the idea. Is this going anywhere?"

"Be patient, Alex. I want you to understand."

"I think I understand," I said with a hint of irony which sailed right over her head.

"He told me he would leave his wife and we would live together, free, together by choice, not by law."

"Natalya, this is of no interest at all to me or to the Mossad."

"But you don't understand. In our love and our relationship he felt liberated, and he began to share some parts of his work with me."

A couple of waiters arrived with our food.

When they had left, I raised both hands like she was holding a gun on me.

"Just hold on a minute, Natalya. When we spoke to you earlier, you told a very convincing story about how you went to see him to tell him it was over and you were returning to Israel and you were done. You were very convincing in the telling, too. But now you're telling me the exact opposite, and you are equally convincing. You know what happens to really skilled liars, don't you, Natalya? Nobody believes a damned word they say."

She sat staring into her plate. "You are so brutal," she said again, then gestured at me with her open hand. "Oh, yes, very refined and elegant, but this is just a veneer for the animal that lies underneath."

"I am not here to have a discussion about my primal character, and I am not here to have you describe your intimate relationship with Dr. Geller. Now cut the amateur dramatics and tell me why I should believe a damned word you say or why I should be here at all."

"I am very afraid."

"You said that."

"Please, let me speak."

I was about to tell her to say something worth listening to but held back, and she went on.

"When David was killed, it was a terrible shock for me, and I realized quickly that I was probably the last person to see him before the killer himself. I was almost in panic, and I thought the best thing would be for me to say he and I had finished. I was in such a state it did not cross my mind that the separation could be a motive, especially if I was leaving him!" She waved a hand at her face. "My emotion was not hard to fake. It was not fake. You just attributed it to wrong motives."

She poked at her food with her fork for a bit. "But when you came, I saw you are a good man—a brute, but you are honest. I knew I could not betray David. To betray Israel is to betray David, and not telling you what he shared with me, that is to betray Israel."

She speared a piece of lettuce and put it in her mouth.

I sighed and cut into the steak. "So what did he tell you, Natalya?"

"He had found proof."

"Proof? Proof of what?"

"Proof of a cabal. It has a structure, headquarters, levels of membership, a leader—everything. He knows who are the members, he knows who is the leader. He is the king of the world. His word is law."

I shook my head. "No, Natalya. I don't believe it. It's science fiction, fantasy. Those things don't happen in the real world." I gave a small laugh. "I know because I work in the places where that kind of thing would happen, and it doesn't."

There was something odd in her expression like bitter amusement but more bitter than amused.

"You stupid people," she said to her plate. "You live in a dream. You do not see that everything is a lie."

She placed a small piece of fish in her mouth and watched me while she chewed. The only reason I hadn't gotten up to leave was because I could see Nero scowling at me in my mind, and it was making me uneasy.

"I am going to ask you a favor, Alex. I am going to tell you a short story, and when I am finished, I want you to tell me again that these things do not happen in real life."

I sighed and spread my hands and cut into my steak again. She started talking.

"Some years ago, in the 1940s or '50s, two young men met. I think it was in Los Angeles, but I am not sure. They were talented and intelligent and had lots of imagination, and they began to write for magazines like *Astounding Stories* and others. It was at the time Asimov was doing the same thing.

"Soon, the stories they were writing began to go to their heads and affect their thinking. Perhaps they were taking hallu-cinogens, I don't know. Eventually one of them had the idea to go into the desert, do a ritual, and invoke the goddess Babalon on Earth. He did this because he was the high priest, in United States, of the magical system of Thelema, established by Aleister Crowley. It was Aleister Crowley who personally asked him to become master of the American branch. Eventually his wife betrayed him with his best friend, they stole all of his money and abandoned him, and his friend established a church that became so powerful millionaires and billionaires, people powerful enough to influence presidents and governments, joined, became members. Do you know who these people are?"

I sighed again, more loudly. "No, Natalya, I don't."

"The man who invoked Babalon was Jack Parsons, the founder of the Jet Propulsion Laboratory and consultant to Israel on their rocket program. And his closest friend, who stole his wife and his money and founded that church, was L. Ron Hubbard, the father of Scientology, which even today ministers to some of the richest, most powerful people in the world."

I sat and stared at her. She paused, watching me back. "Actually," she said at last, "I have two questions for you, Alex. They are related. First, if all I have told you happened around 1945 to 1950, how hard would it be to accept and believe that Thelema and Skull and Bones were related in some way? Considering that one of your recent presidents' grandmothers spent time as a guest at the same house in Paris as Aleister Crowley, how hard would it be to believe there was a connection between the secret rituals of Skull and Bones and the secret rituals of Thelema?" She gave me a moment. When I said nothing, she went on. "My second question, Alex: Would you like to tell me again that these things don't happen in the corridors of power—in the world of the Military Industrial Intelligence Complex?"

I could feel my brain groan inside my head. "Are you telling me that Aleister Crowley's cult of Thelema, Skull and Bones, and the Scientologists are trying to take over the world? Natalya, I am not stupid—"

"No! I am not saying that! For God's sake, Alex! Stop being the man who knows everything and is never wrong. There is a lot at stake here, and you need to listen!"

"Well, for Christ's sake say something worth listening to!"

"I am trying to make you see something. If you believe that highly intelligent, motivated people do not slip into ritualistic mysticism in the pursuit of power, then you are blind! The whole political history of the world is tied up with ritualistic mysticism! How do you think religions get invented? People need rituals, and highly intelligent people need big, complex, mystical rituals! What is Sunday mass if not a ritual to invoke the power of Yahweh?"

A couple of people at neighboring tables glanced over. She took a deep breath and lowered her voice.

"I am telling you that he had found proof that this cabal existed. I am not saying they sacrificed children or any of that crazy shit. But just as we know Skull and Bones exists, just as we know Jack Parson was involved in Crowley's Thelema, just as we know that Oppenheimer, Einstein, and Newton were involved in different types of mysticism—this cabal exists, and it has drawn to it the most powerful people on the planet." She spread her hands and shook her head, like I made even less sense than the crazy stuff she was telling me. "If you are here with Captain Gallin, investigating all this, surely you must know something about the nature of the research he was conducting with Dr. Orlev! Is what I am saying not consistent with what you know?"

"Can you give me the names?"

"Some of them. Alex, when he told me this, it was at the same time that we were confessing our feelings for each other. It was a crazy time, and if I am honest, I was as skeptical as you are now. So I remember some of the names, but only some."

"Natalya, did he show you any *real* evidence?"

"He did more than that. He showed me proof."

NINE

I LEANED BACK IN MY CHAIR AND COCKED AN
eyebrow at her. "Proof? What kind of proof?"

"There was a mole. A general who had been national security advisor to three presidents. He had been a man of action, a
warrior, a Christian of solid protestant faith, a man of God. He
became a member of the cabal because his father had been a
member. They were an old, Anglo-Scandinavian family from
New York who had become wealthy and influential through
wise, far-sighted investments and had pulled out of the stock
market just before it collapsed in 1929."

"Does this family have a name, or do I just have to take
your word for it?"

"General William H. Drake."

"General William Drake?" Geller's wife had mentioned
that name too. He had been a fixture at the White House for
almost fifteen years.

"That's what I am telling you, Alex. He was deeply
involved in the cabal when he was younger, but as he got older,

he began to doubt its motives and regret his involvement. This is what David told me."

"You said he showed you proof."

She glanced over my shoulder and around the dining room. "He did, but—"

I said, "Wait, we can't discuss this here." I pulled out my cell and called Nero. After they'd put me through voice recognition, his voice said, "Tell me."

I grinned at Natalya, like I was including her in a family chat.

"Hey Mom, listen, we're here out on the town in London, and we were wondering, I've had a couple of drinks and I really don't fancy the drive back. Could we stay in your London pad?"

"Who are you with?"

"Oh, she's great and she sends her love. Say hi to Mom, Natty! She sent a kiss."

"You are a clown, Alex."

"I *know!* Isn't it great?"

"What is the level of risk?"

"Oh, hi Dad! Hi! Natty says hi too. And I could use a car. The price of taxi cabs in London is crazy!"

"Understood. 110 B Cheyne Walk. I'll talk to the London office. You should have someone with you in ten to twenty minutes. They should tell you..." He sighed, and there might have been the ghost of a trace of a shadow of a smile in his voice. "They should tell you Mom sent them."

"Bye, Mom, love you too!"

Natalya had stopped with her glass halfway to her mouth when I had started talking. Her eyes were narrowed. Now she sipped and set her glass down on the table.

"You are a strange man. Perhaps in another life you could have been talented."

"Yeah." I shrugged. "You know what Sun Tzu said."

She laughed, and for a moment she looked beautiful. "No!" she said. "I have no idea what Sun Tzu said, or who Sun Tzu is!"

"He was a Chinese philosopher. He wrote *The Art of War*, and he said, 'Be extremely subtle, even to the point of formlessness. Be extremely mysterious, even to the point of soundlessness. Thereby you can be the director of your opponent's fate."

She stared at me a moment longer, then nodded at her glass. "Strange man. Strange man."

A little later, two young men came in asking for a table for two. One of them looked over and spread his hands.

"Al? Al, me old mate! Imagine meeting you here!" He came over as I stood, laughing. "Son of a gun! Small world! How's it hangin'?"

He gave me a hug, and I felt the car fob and the house keys slip into my pocket. He pointed at Natalya. "Natty? Beautiful as ever. I didn't see you hiding there in the corner. You just arrived? Can we join you?"

"Actually, we were just leaving. You want our table?' I called over to the waiter. "They can have our table."

We did a lot of back slapping, said a lot of *call me*s, Natalya got a few more kisses than was perhaps strictly necessary, and we left the restaurant. As we stepped through the door, I pressed the button on the fob, and a Grenadier three cars down bleeped. The Ineos Grenadier is a tank lightly disguised as a four-by-four, and this one was probably bullet-proof and bomb-proof. I smiled, scanned the road, as they had probably done when they arrived, and led Natalya to the passenger seat.

It was a short drive down Fulham Road. I took it easy, moving with the pulse of the traffic from traffic light to traffic light along the wet blacktop under the colored lights and the dreary glow of the all-night corner shops. The rain had eased to a drizzle, and the wipers scraped and clocked as and when they remembered to.

I pulled up at the lights beside the Sokol Book Store, on the corner of Old Church Street. The wipers squeaked across the windshield.

"So tell me about General William H. Drake."

"He is a patriotic man, a man of honor. He knows the danger of Russian imperialism. He knows that the specter of Soviet Imperialism still haunts the Russian elite. It is alive and possesses Putin's black soul, and it has now found a spiritual home in Islam, in Iran."

The lights changed from a wet red to a mouthwatering green, and I took off nice and steady, scanning my mirrors and turning left into Old Church Street.

"That's nice," I said. "Have you any actual information to go with that, or am I just going to get your subjective opinion?"

"Always the brute. I am trying to explain to you, make you understand what kind of man he is. History, Alex, is not driven by events. History is a series of events that are driven by unique personalities that take action."

"OK, but let me know when we are done with the theory. Because, Natalya, we are very short of time."

" I know, but you have to understand that General Drake is not a traitor. He heard, somehow, because of the position he holds at the heart of American national security, he heard about the research which the Mossad had commissioned from

David and—this is what David told me—he approached David privately and told him he can provide information."

We had reached the river beside the Chelsea Old Church. There was no traffic, so I pulled out and turned right. We cruised along beside the Thames, watching the lights warp and ripple on the water. Natalya gazed at it and spoke more to herself than to me.

"It is an ancient river," she said, "but the water in it is always brand new."

It was just three or four hundred yards to the house. As I pulled over and killed the lights, I looked at her and said, "And if you make a hole in a net, there are less holes than you started with. When we go through that door, you start giving me some useful information or I am putting you out on your fanny. I canceled a flight to come and talk to you because you said you had information for me. Now you either give it to me, or you give it to the boys at the Mossad in Tel Aviv. You choose."

It was a three-story 1930s redbrick with sash windows, an attic, and a small front yard behind iron railings. I pushed open the gate, and she moved in down the path. I scanned the road in both directions, but I was pretty sure nobody had followed us. I unlocked the door, then gently pushed her inside.

It was dark. It smelled of furniture polish and stale air. I closed the door and switched on the light to find her two inches from me, looking up into my face.

"Will you take me? I feel so alone and frightened."

"Cut it out, Natalya." I pointed to a door on the right. "Go in the living room, sit down, and stay away from the windows. You want coffee?"

She moved to the door and opened it, then turned back to

me like I'd told her Santa didn't exist. "I want coffee," she said and pushed through the door.

I followed her through, found the kitchen at the back, made some coffee, and found a bottle of Bells in with the baked beans and the rice. I carried all that out and found her sitting at the small melamine dining table at the back of the room. She looked up as I set the tray on the table.

"We are at the end of history," she told me. She seemed to have a genius for making huge statements that didn't actually mean anything. I tried not to sigh, sat, and poured. "Why's that?" I asked and wished I hadn't.

"It is what David has told me, and it is what General Drake has told him. This is the end of history. You think I am being a drama queen, but it is what he said."

"OK, Natalya, let's get down to brass tacks. I am going to ask you some questions, and you are going to answer them as though you were writing an academic paper, covering all the points and no emotional fluff. You got it?"

"I've got it."

"I want the names, all the names you know, of the members of the cabal."

"Well, let's start with the presidents of the United States."

"Come on, Natalya, I'm losing patience."

She pointed at me across the table. "What does it take for evil to prosper, Alex? What does it take? It takes for good men to look the other way. Some of your presidents since Eisenhower have been complicit, others have looked the other way, but none, save Eisenhower and Kennedy made any effort to stop the spread of evil which Truman unknowingly unleashed."

"What are you talking about?"

"Have you *heard* of the National Security Act? Have you *heard* of the Octopus Murders? Are you aware that the president at the time knew of the murders and their connection with Iran-Contra? Did you know that the Justice Department, operating through the NSA and the CIA, had people imprisoned and murdered to stop the story getting out?"

"OK, Natalya, I can get all this bullshit on a hundred sites on Google—"

"Alex! Wake up! Your country is not run by the president, the White House, or Congress. Your country is run by the Pentagon in partnership with the major defense and IT contractors, and you *know* this!"

I sighed. "Names."

"I know five names, and I can guess five more."

"*Tell me!*"

"Ben J. Hyder, the chief executive officer of Norman Swirbul Space and Aeronautics Corporation. Mitch Hansen, CEO of Skyhawk Defense Technology Corporation, Abraham Bellow, director of the Rat Labs, William Portos, the founder of the Portal Operating System used universally by the military, law enforcement, and banks worldwide, and Richard Bramble, the former director of Central Intelligence. There are many more, but in addition to these, you can count at least five former presidents."

"This is insane."

"They call themselves the Cabal, or sometimes the Family. They are above the law. They will perpetrate any crime with impunity, and there is no way to get to them because they control the organs of government and through them the agencies of law enforcement."

I stood and walked to the window. Through the thin gap

between the drapes, I could see the liquid lights bobbing and twisting on the river. The black water was tinted amber here and there by the street lamps.

"Geller said he had proof of this?"

"He said he had conclusive proof. He had gathered a lot of compelling evidence, and when General Drake came forward, he was able to make it conclusive. But he suspected that the Cabal had learned of his association with the general and had decided to kill them both. So he passed everything he had to his friend."

I turned to face her. "Who runs this? Who is at the head of this? I can't believe something like this can be sustained. It would collapse under its own weight. It's fantasy, science fiction."

"Elroy Harrison, the former governor of Nevada. He controls everything."

I stared at her, telling myself she was crazy. "Who has the research now?"

"I don't know."

"You don't know or you're afraid to tell me?"

"Alex! I have come here voluntarily to give you this information. I put my own life at risk to help you! Why be hostile to me?"

I sighed and rubbed my face, then ran my fingers through my hair. "I'm sorry, Natalya. This is all pretty hard to swallow. I need to talk to General Drake."

I thought about Nero. He had specifically told us to limit our investigation to finding the flash drive. If I asked him to set up a meeting with Drake, he was liable to take us off the case. I looked at Natalya and studied her face a moment.

"Can you swing that?"

"A meeting with Drake?"

"Do you know him? Does he know about you?"

She hesitated. "We met once, in Tel Aviv. He came incognito, via the Israeli Embassy in Washington, DC."

"Can you contact him? Can you arrange a meeting?"

"I will try. What shall I tell him?"

In my mind, Nero's massive shadow loomed over me. His eyes burned me from under beetling brows.

"Tell him a close friend and ally of Professor Geller's needs his help."

"All right, I will do that. But Alex, what am I to do? My life is in danger. I don't know who to trust."

"I'll tell you. This is what we are going to do. I am going to talk to Captain Gallin and explain to her that you are helping us and you are under my protection. OK? She will transmit that to the Mossad. And right now, I am going to take you to the Israeli Embassy and put you in the care of my old friend Gabriel Gallin. He will take care of you."

"Gallin?"

"Her father. Trust me, they are good people."

She protested a lot, but I called Gallin, explained the situation, and got her to talk to her father. About half an hour later, we set off again in the Grenadier for Hyde Park and Palace Green.

It was getting late. The temperature had dropped, and the rain had started in again. Warwick Road was practically empty, slick and glistening with wet light as I headed north through the night. In my rearview mirror, I could see the headlamps of a car behind us. It kept its distance, but it stayed with us as far as The Cromwell Road. There it peeled off west, but was immediately replaced by another car out of the Tesco parking lot on

Fenelon Place. That one stayed with me onto Kensington High Street all the way to Church Street. It might have been just some guy, but I couldn't take the risk of letting him see me turn in to the Embassy. So I pulled in like I was turning into a narrow, one-way alley at Kensington Church Court. He passed, and I waited till he'd disappeared from view before reversing back onto the High Street and heading for Palace Green and the Israeli Embassy.

TEN

Gallin and her father, Gabriel, had met us at the Embassy. I had handed Natalya over, and they had taken her into protective custody. We had then spent half an hour talking with Gabriel before getting back in the Grenadier, pulling out of the security barrier, and turning right onto Church Street.

She gave me a sidelong once-over. "So was it all work, or did you get a bit of play too?"

I gave her the kind of baleful look Nero could use to bring dangerous men to their knees. It made Gallin grin. I said, "Work."

"Useful?"

I filled her in as we climbed the hill and turned left into Notting Hill Gate. When I was done I told her, "I have asked her to arrange a meeting with General Drake."

"When for?"

"As soon as possible."

"Have you forgotten we're going to Menorca and you have

promised me dinner somewhere nice in Mahon if I wore a cute dress?"

"Of course not."

"Good because I packed your bag, and the ODIN Gulfstream is on standby at City Airport."

"OK. I was followed here. I shook him, but they're watching us."

"No problem. I'll drive to the airport."

I felt a stab of irritation. "I can shake a tail, Gallin."

"Yeah. Not like me you can't." She grinned and punched my shoulder. "Loosen up, big guy. We got this."

I glanced at her, shook my head, and sighed. "Like Noah and Naamah had it. The most we can look forward to, Gallin, is to survive in the remote north as one of a handful of breeding couples, while the elite drink martinis and champagne in environmentally controlled domes, served by servile androids."

"Us? A breeding couple? Are you out of your mind? Can you imagine what our kids would be like? They'd be homicidal maniacs."

I nodded. "Therein lies the last hope for humanity."

"You have to stop talking to sexy Russian academics who moonlight as skilled international assassins."

I ignored her, staring out of the windshield at the darkness of Holland Park Avenue until we came to Campden Hill Square. As I turned in, I said, "We are doing precisely what Nero told us not to do. When this is over, you go back to the Mossad, but I am finished."

I pulled up outside her house, and we sat in silence for a moment.

"What do you want to do?" she asked, then added, "We're going to Menorca to recover the drive. That's it."

"The inquiries we've made, Dr. Ivanova, the involvement of the Israeli Embassy..." I sighed.

"We had no choice, Mason. There was no other way to do it."

"Explain that to him."

"OK, then that's what we'll do. We get in there, we collect our bags, and we have a conference with Nero. We tell him. I'll tell him. He can't penalize you for this. There was too much at stake, and we had to take whatever steps were necessary. Period."

I nodded and sighed. "OK, let's go talk to him."

Inside, she made some coffee while I arranged the meeting, and twenty minutes later we were sitting looking at Nero's huge head framed in my laptop while he sipped a glass of cognac. Gallin cut right in.

"Sir, you have given us an impossible mission."

There was absolutely no humor in his face when he said, "It is what I have come to expect of you. Like that television show when I was a boy."

"That's cute sir, really, it is. But, see, it's not actually the *mission* that's impossible."

"You had better explain yourself, Captain."

He sipped, and she sighed. "We think we have located the drive, and we believe we can close in and recover it by tomorrow or the day after..." She paused, and he arched an eyebrow. "However, in order to obtain the intelligence that led us to this point, I had to disregard your orders. Mason tried to stop me, but I had deduced just how perilous this situation was for Israel, and I had no choice but to question Israeli academics regarding the nature of the report the Mossad had commissioned from Dr. Geller." They stared at each other a while, and the force between them was a palpable thing. Finally she said, very quietly, "With the greatest respect, being an agent of the Mossad, being an Israeli officer, operating in Israel with other Israelis, I believe I was acting outside your jurisdiction, sir. If you decide to terminate my secondment, I will understand; however, I would stress that there is nobody on the planet better placed than me to help Mason bring this to a satisfactory conclusion."

He sipped his cognac and set the glass very carefully down before him. I narrowed my eyes and peered hard at the screen. For a moment, I could have sworn I saw the faint glimmer of a shadow of the ghost of a smile at the corner of his mouth.

"I had promised those who brief and instruct me," he said, gazing down, presumably at his glass which was out of view, "that I would not allow anyone to acquaint themselves with the contents of that drive. However, as you have so clearly pointed out, Captain, you were acting outside my jurisdiction, and it was wholly beyond my power to stop you. Presumably you have briefed Mr. Mason on the contents?"

Now he raised his eyes to meet hers. She said, "Yes. It was a judgment call. I believe he needs to know if we are to avert a global catastrophe."

"Then I hereby bind you both to the most absolute secrecy. Nobody outside of the two of you must know what is on that drive."

She said, "Understood. You have my word."

"Alex?"

"You have my word, sir. Consider me bound."

"I do. So where is the drive, and what are your next steps?"

I told him, "We believe it's still on Menorca. We think Peter may have gone to ground."

"Your reasons?"

"In the first place, Peter had killed Orlev's assassin and taken the drive. It is very unlikely the Cabal would have sent two assassins, and if they had, they would both have been at the house. In the second place, I have been followed, and Dr. Ivanova—Geller's lover—believes she has been followed too and was in fear for her life. If they had killed Peter and already had the drive, they wouldn't be wasting their time following us. They'd be keeping the lowest profile they could."

He grunted. "Perhaps."

"Whether I am right or wrong, sir, there is a chance Peter is still on the island hoping the penny will drop and we'll go and get him. It is suggestive that a body has not yet shown up."

"Agreed. Anything else?"

Gallin said, "Yeah. Dr. Ivanova was in fear for her life. We weren't clear who we could trust within the UK or US, so we put her in the care of Gabriel at the Israeli Embassy."

"Very well."

"But you need to talk to Gabriel because it looks like Geller had talked to her."

I cut in. "He gave her a list of the five names of the five leading members of the Cabal."

"Dear God, that man...!"

"Mitch Hansen, CEO of the Skyhawk Defense Technology Corporation, Abraham Bellow, director of the Rat Labs, William Portos, the founder of the Portal Operating System, Richard Bramble, the former director of the CIA, Ben J. Hyder, the chief executive officer of Norman Swirbul Space and Aeronautics Corporation, and add to them Elroy Harrison, the former Governor of Nevada. He is apparently the head honcho. She also said there were five recent presidents who were members and she talked a lot of crap about Aleister Crowley, Thelema and Skull and Bones."

He remained very quiet, looking to one side as his lips twitched. Finally he took a deep breath, grunted, and sighed. "Go to Menorca. Find Peter Blakelock and recover the drive. Forget everything. I will institute damage limitation measures."

"Sir," I blurted out, "is there *any* truth in all this sci-fi crap?"

He stared at me for a long time. Finally he said, "Truth. It is all lies. All of it. Everything you have ever been taught or told is a *lie!*"

And he killed the connection.

We sat and stared at the dead screen for a long moment. Then we sat and stared at each other in silence until Gallin said, "Son of a bitch."

I stood. "Come on. Let's get going."

We took our bags out to the Cerbera, slung them on the tiny back seat, and took off for the airport. The drive was harrowing but uneventful, and an hour later, we were soaring over the English Channel, headed south toward the Mediterranean. Gallin was nursing a martini while I toyed with a coffee.

"There's something that has been playing on my mind," I told her.

She was gazing out of the window at the passing clouds reflecting the moonlight. "We are not going to be a breeding couple, Mason. Forget it."

"Let's be positive," I said, ignoring her, "and assume we

find Peter and recover the drive and hand both over safely to Nero."

She shifted her gaze from the window to my face and frowned.

"OK..."

"What happens next? Nero said he was engaging in damage limitation. What does that mean? These bastards get away with whatever they have been doing? What, exactly, have they been doing? Are we entitled to know? Do the people—the people of the Western, democratic world—do they get to know about what's been going on for the last seventy-odd years?"

She gave a soft grunt and turned her gaze back to the window. I went on.

"I mean, what are we talking about here? Is this organized crime on a grand scale or a political coup the likes of which nobody has ever seen before? Are we talking about a bunch of crazies triggering a war in the Middle East so it will benefit their oil interests, or are we talking about a bunch of crazies actually engineering society so that democracy itself withers and dies?"

"I don't know."

"Because if that's what it is, Gallin, I want to know why Nero is engaged in damage limitation instead of doing everything in his power to destroy this cabal."

"We'd better ask him."

"Yeah? I don't know."

Her frown deepened. "What do you mean?"

"I mean neither of us got to mention General William Drake to him before he had his tantrum and switched off his computer."

"Huh..." She scratched her head. "Am I thinking what you're thinking?"

"I hope so. Because if what Drake has is as conclusive and explosive as Natalya Ivanova says it is, that shit needs to hit the fan. We don't want damage limitation, we want all-out devastation."

"Oh, man. You are on a very dangerous train of thought there, big guy."

"If what they are telling us is true, we can't just sweep it under the carpet. If General Drake can hurt them, really hurt them, we have to enable him to do it."

"But we need to talk to Nero first, Mason."

"Yeah? If he's running damage limitation, what do you think he's going to tell us to do?"

"Nothing."

"Right."

"Shit!" She said it quietly and turned her attention to the moonlit clouds again.

"You know I'm right."

She didn't answer. After a while, she finished her drink and closed her eyes. I finished my coffee and tried to do the same, but Nero's words kept echoing in my mind. Nero was one of the two or three people I most admired and respected on the planet. But you can't trust anyone one hundred percent. Apart from anything else, it's not fair on them. We all have the right to be fallible. And Nero shouldered a massive responsibility as the head of ODIN. From where he sat, I could see that damage limitation might be the only sane thing to do. If what we had heard from our witnesses was true, the impact of what was on the flash drive could be seismic. It could bring the whole structure of Western society to its knees.

But from where I was sitting, to cover up this conspiracy and allow these people to go free, wielding the power they wielded, harboring the intentions they harbored, was unthinkable. If the structure of our world was truly this rotten, if we were moving toward a dystopia where people were exploited like androids, better to burn it down and rebuild it than allow the parasites to keep feeding on it and infecting it with their disease. And with those thoughts in my mind, I drifted into a troubled sleep.

We stepped out into the cold parking lot. It was the darkest hour before the dawn. A biting wind was coming in off the ocean, and I paused a moment and shivered, glancing up at the sky, but the glare from the airport had obliterated all but the brightest stars. Gallin stopped a little way ahead of me with the fob in her hand. A Jeep a little farther down bleeped. She turned back, dangling the fob from her fingers, watching me. The smile surprised me. I smiled back.

She said, "We've covered a lot of ground, huh, big guy, since Manila. Remember the Peak Grill at the Grand Hyatt?"

"How could I forget?"

She pointed at me, laughing. "You had your James Bond evening suit with the satin lapels."

"You were in a completely immoral red velvet cocktail dress."[1]

She grinned. "You fancied me."

I was going to deny it, but something in my gut told me it would be a mistake. I raised my shoulders a fraction of an inch. "Yeah, well, you clean up good, Gallin."

The smile faded from her lips slightly. "Yeah? You looked pretty good yourself." She came back a couple of steps and linked her arm through mine, and we walked the short distance

---

1. See *Alex Mason One, Odin*

toward the Jeep. "It hasn't been long, but it feels like a whole lifetime, huh?"

I gave a small laugh. "I used to have girlfriends. Now it's just you and Manny Pacquiao."

She looked up into my face, and there was gentle laughter in her eyes. "That's not a bad trade, Mason, and you know it."

We stopped at the truck, and she moved around to the driver's side. There she stopped and leaned on the hood.

"Tell me the truth, Mason. Are we going to be OK? How bad is this going to get? Is this like..." She shook her head. "Like the *Apocalypse?*"

I was gripped, probably for the first time in my life, by a sudden and overpowering need to be truly honest. Not just to tell the truth, but to mean it and communicate my feelings. I dropped my bag and moved around the hood of the Jeep, taking hold of Gallin's hands in mine. My thoughts on the flight were mixing in a volatile cocktail with feelings I didn't properly understand.

"Gallin, I am not a religious man, but if Revelation really is a prophetic text, then the Apocalypse has already begun. Things could get dark from here on in, but I want you to know something. I need you to know something. I will always..."

Her frown had deepened, like I'd started speaking Greek and she was having trouble translating. It was a split second. Then there was a voice calling. It was a man's voice, and I felt a jolt of anger at his intrusion. Gallin turned and looked. The voice called again, "Mason? Mr. Alex Mason?"

I turned. There was a shadow approaching, maybe thirty yards away, backlit by the glare from the airport. I didn't answer. I raised my hand to shade my eyes from the glare and saw him stop. Too late I realized what was happening. Gallin's scream filled my head. I felt her body jolt hard against mine. Then a searing heat filled my chest.

ELEVEN

I OPENED MY EYES. A DARK SKY STRETCHED TO infinity overhead, pierced by one or two silver stars. A cold breeze touched my skin. I saw grayness near the horizon. Dawn was coming. Very far away there were voices. I was oddly aware they were too far away, too far to do anything, too far to help. There was an intense pain in my chest, and I knew I was dying, yet I felt strangely at peace. I closed my eyes and allowed myself to sink away from the pain, into the dark stillness.

The stillness was timeless. Sometimes a voice in my head said that the stillness was healing me, mending the damage, fixing the wounds. At other times, a different voice told me I was feverish and incoherent, and I should prepare myself for the transition. Then I would sink deeper into a world of empty blackness, where my mind was quiet. It was a good place where there was no pain and no anxiety. But it was a state that could not last. Something was nagging at me. Something, a voice in my head told me, which would not let me pass.

It was not my time.

I opened my eyes and saw sunlight in a window. There was a man frowning at me. He looked old with gray hair and Gandalf eyebrows. I tried to talk, to ask, but all I could manage was to draw air into my lungs.

The old guy said, "What?"

I moved my mouth. He took hold of a plastic bottle with a tube and stuck it in my mouth. I felt water squirt from the tube and swallowed it gratefully. He removed the tube and I croaked, "Gallin..."

Movement, a scrape, a figure loomed against the bright square of the window. Gallin. She looked mad and was scowling at me. I smiled weakly. I felt a prick in my arm, closed my eyes, and sank back into the deep blackness.

The pain had changed. Now it was an ache. It was everywhere, and however I moved, it was still there. There was no way to stop it. It occupied me, all of me. I heard myself groan. Twisted, tried to open my eyes. Hands held me, raised my head. I tasted water and drank deep. Then slipped back into blessed darkness.

A voice said, "Apocalypse," and I knew I was dreaming. A man with a long, white beard and a skullcap was telling a group of people: "Apocalypse is disclosure in ancient Greek. In Hebrew we say har Megiddo. Har Megiddo. You remember Megiddo. Har Megiddo. Armageddon."

IT WAS DAWN, and my eyes were open. Through the window, I could see the Mediterranean, and the sky was turning from gray to pale blue, streaked with red. Gallin was asleep in an armchair by the window. I lay for a while without moving as copper light touched the sky and leaned in through the window to rest on her cheek. When it touched her eyelids, she blinked, looked about her, saw I was awake, and sat up.

Her first word was, "Asshole." Then she smiled. "Do you know how much you scared me?"

I didn't have the strength for a witty riposte, so I just smiled. After a moment, I asked, "Are you OK? You look OK."

"I'm OK."

I spoke slowly, sleepily. "Where are we? I guess I took a slug, huh? Did you get the guy? How long have you been here?"

"Slow down, big guy. One little step at a time. We've been here about twenty-four hours."

I paused, enjoying the sight of her, then asked, "Where is here?"

She stared at me a long time, then smiled. "Peter Blakelock's villa."

I closed my eyes and groaned. "*What?* My brain hurts."

"He'll explain it to you. It actually makes the kind of weird-ass sense that Nero makes when he talks." She paused and looked out the window. "Mason, that guy was gunning for you. He called out your name."

"I know. I heard him." I hesitated. "Gallin, when you pushed me..."

"Stop."

"No."

"Don't make this weird."

"You put yourself in the path of the bullet. If you had pushed me half a second earlier, you would have been shot."

She sighed. "Yeah, well, that just shows how shit hot my timing is."

I made a rueful smile. "Thanks, but please don't do that again. I need you alive."

"Shut up, Mason. I am no use to you alive if you're dead."

I closed my eyes a moment before asking, "Did you get the guy?" I opened my eyes again. She shook her head. I frowned. "How come?"

"I thought you were dead."

She said it like it was an explanation. I frowned harder in a way that asked how that made a difference. She looked away, out of the window again.

"You were lucky I pushed you. He was a damned good shot. He would have got you square in the heart. As it is, you'll have an ugly scar for the rest of your life in your left pectoral. It's a miracle it didn't tear the tendon clean off. There was a lot of blood."

"You let him get away so you could stop the bleeding."

"He ran. Don't you dream of lecturing me. I had my priorities straight. You would have done the same."

She was right. "I'm not in a hospital. I'm in Blakelock's villa. What happened?" "Blakelock was at the airport."

I shook my head. "No. That's too much of a coincidence."

"It wasn't a coincidence. He was waiting for us."

"Bullshit."

"Will you shut up? It was exactly as you thought, asshole. He was watching London and Washington flights, hoping, as you said he would, that the penny would drop. He recognized you and followed us out to the parking lot. He was about to approach us, but the other guy got there first."

I grunted and thought about it for a moment. "Is that the first time you have ever told me I was right?" She didn't say anything. She just looked at me like she was wondering where to hit me. "I know it's not the first time you've called me an asshole. But I think it's the first time you've said, 'Mason, you were right.'"

"Mason, you need to get serious."

"Yeah, but I'm wounded."

"How did the gunman know we would be here? More to the point: how did he know *you* would be here?"

I sighed. "Gallin, I just woke up from what I presume was basic, household surgery. You make a very valid point, but my brain can't cope with it right now."

She didn't smile. "Mason, you *need* to cope. Right now."

"OK, I'll cope, but like your great aunt used to say, 'I'll cope, but first I'll eat!'" She sat and stared at me. She still looked like she wanted to hit me. I said, "What? A coffee and a piece of toast is too much to ask for a wounded man? It's not a lot to ask..." Then it dawned on me, and I mouthed, *You think Pete alerted the Cabal?*

"No." She leaned forward. "But I might have! Now pull yourself together!"

She stood, and I frowned. She had tears in her eyes. In a sudden rush, she bent down and gave me a painful hug. Then slammed out of the room saying something about getting coffee.

While she was gone, I lay and stared at the ceiling considering how weird women were and how surreal the situation was. Then I practiced moving my shoulder. The pain was intense but tolerable. Fortunately, it was my left shoulder. Using my right arm, I eased myself up into a sitting position and thought about getting out of bed. However, the thought of Gallin coming back with coffee and toast made me wonder whether, if I played the pathetic card a little longer, I might get another hug. I figured I'd get up after breakfast.

She returned fifteen minutes later with a plate of eggs, bacon and sausages, a basket of croissants, and a large cup of black coffee. She also brought Blakelock with her and an old guy with Gandalf eyebrows.

Blakelock nodded once at me. "Mason. You gave us a scare. This is Doc Holliday. He fixed you up."

I gave him a smile. "I feel I should make some wisecrack about Wyatt Earp, but my brain ain't there yet. Thanks."

"Don't thank me. Thank Peter and Ms. Gallin. If she hadn't given you that shove, that slug would have punched a hole right through your heart. And if Peter hadn't gotten you here at the hurry up, you'd have bled out for sure. I've given you a transfusion and stitched you up. But that won't fix you. What's going to fix you is giving your body the chance to heal." He pointed at my plate of bacon and eggs. "And plenty of protein." He gave his head a little shake. "I don't know what your job is, sir, but whatever it is, get somebody else to do it. You need rest."

He turned to Blakelock. "Peter, let me know if you need anything. I'll see myself out."

He left and closed the door behind him. Gallin sat in the armchair by the window, and Blakelock pulled up a straight-back chair beside the bed. Before he could say anything, I said, "It's good to see you alive. Everyone assumed you were dead."

He nodded, then gave a small shrug. "That was a risk. But using any kind of technology was a bigger risk. The people we are up against are formidable."

"How do you know that?"

He didn't bat an eyelid. "Because I'm not stupid, Mason.

After I found Orlev with toothpicks under his nails, I began to put two and two together. There was Nero's absolute prohibition on inquiring into the contents of the drive, there was the caliber of the men working on it—Geller and Orlev, there was Orlev's drunken ramblings... By the time I got back to Mahon from Orlev's house, I knew I was in well over my head, and I went to ground."

"You went to ground by renting a villa?"

He laughed. "I know Menorca quite well. I used to come here a lot at one time. Besides, isn't it what Nero is always telling us? They'll always look for you in cheap motels and hostels. Nobody will ever look for you at the Ritz. Like all of us, I have my escape resources. So I rented a villa in the name of John Smith and hid in plain view, hoping that someone back home would realize our enemy wasn't going to send two men to get Orlev, and if they had they would have seen to me at Orlev's house." I gave Gallin a smug smile. Blakelock added, "It seems you thought that very thing, and I am extremely grateful to you."

"The gratitude is mutual," I told him. "But I'm afraid our primary mission was not to come and get you. That was a bonus. Nero sent us to find the drive."

There was a hint of irony in his smile. "I am aware of that."

"You have it?"

He shook his head. "I can't give you a straight answer to that right now, Mason—"

"Why the hell not?"

"Just bear with me and hear me out."

"Hear you out? Where's the damned flash drive, Peter?"

Gallin's voice came softly from the window. "Hear him

out, Mason. We've already had this conversation, and he has a point."

"*What point?*"

"If you'll shut up, he'll tell you."

"This better be good, Blakelock."

He gave me a look that said he was trying not to get mad. "Tell me something. What do you think the Cabal did when their man never came back from Menorca with the flash drive? What do you think they did when they then discovered, through their widespread channels, that he had been beaten to death with a marble tabletop?"

I took a deep breath. He nodded.

"Right. They started to scour flight manifests for people who might have a link to one of a number of intelligence agencies, including the Mossad, MI6, CIA, and ODIN. And I really want to stress here that we *do not know* how far their tentacles reach. We can be sure Nero is clean, but that's as far as it goes. What we do know now is that they have reached ODIN at some level. Proof of this is that you had an assassin waiting for you at the airport. Who knew you would be here? A small group at ODIN and the Mossad. But the Cabal knew you were coming."

"OK."

"So in view of those simple facts, how smart do you think it would have been for me to keep the drive at the villa?"

"Not real smart. You made your point. So where is it?"

He raised both palms like he was trying to slow me down. "I'm coming to that. First…"

He glanced at Gallin. She said, "I called the office, and they're making discreet inquiries to view the airport parking lot CCTV footage. It's a long shot, but it would be really useful to get that guy and have a chat with him about who sent him and how they knew you would be here."

"OK, but you're right. It is a long shot. Where is the drive?"

He nodded. "In all probability, we'll have to see. Either way, you need to spend a couple of days recovering. Meantime, Aila and I will look into the CCTV footage and also make some discreet inquires at car rental establishments."

I shook my head. "Not going to happen. And I am telling you both that my patience is wearing thin. This is the fourth time I am going to ask you—"

"We cannot risk—"

"What we can't risk is wasting time on this kind of bullshit. We need to get that damned drive to Nero, and we need to get it to him *now!* If you're afraid of poking your nose out of doors, then we'll get a message to him and have him send a damned battle cruiser to collect it. But not another damned day goes by without us having that damned drive in our possession!"

"Mason..."

"Every goddamned day that drive is at large is a day the Cabal grows stronger and its tentacles stretch farther! The answer is *no!*"

"Mason..."

"What?"

"You dodged a bullet by one inch. Your left pectoral muscle is badly damaged. That assassin knows you and knows who you are. If you are seen, they will kill you. And if you're seen with us, you put our lives at risk too. You need to keep a low profile while we deal with the threat. Once we do that, we can leave the island."

I looked at Gallin. She was gazing out the window. She didn't look happy. I said, "Gallin?" She turned to look at me. "Are you part of this?"

She shook her head. "He has a point. I don't know what to think, but you need to hear him out."

I sat forward and spoke quietly. "OK. I have heard you out. Now you hear me out. If I die, if you die, if—God forbid—Gallin dies, that sucks, but it's what we signed up for, Blakelock. If what is on that drive is for real, our lives don't count for shit anyway. We are being driven *relentlessly*, day by day, into a new Dark Ages that will make the last ones look like a week in Las Vegas. Now I am going to tell you one last time. We are going to take the drive to Nero. We have the company jet waiting at the airport, and we are going to collect the drive. We'll take whatever evasive maneuvers we need to take, but we are going to get that damned drive where it belongs. And we are going to do it now."

He smiled on one side of his face and glanced at my bandaged shoulder. "You talk like a man who is in charge of an operation, Mason. But I would say, the condition you're in, you're out of action. So I am going to take charge, and we are going to do things my way. We neutralize the threat before we go."

Gallin spoke quietly. "Where's the drive, Blakelock?"

Her words were accompanied by the soft click of a semi-automatic.

TWELVE

He sighed and leaned back in his chair.

"Put your gun away, Captain. It's not necessary."

"Are you sure? I'm beginning to wonder."

I said, "Where is the drive, Blakelock?" I gave my head a shake. "Whether I get up, stay in bed, or keep a low damned profile, I am having a real problem understanding why you won't tell us where the damned drive is. We are acting directly for Nero, so what's the problem? Where is the damned drive?"

Gallin shifted her Sig so it was aiming at his knee. She didn't say anything. I said, "Don't make us do this, Blakelock."

Anger suffused his face. "You don't need to do it. I saved your life, goddammit! It's at Cala Lucalari. It is impossible for me to explain where." He turned and scowled at Gallin. "Even if you blow my kneecaps off, I'll have to take you there." He turned back to me. "But you are in no condition."

"Cala? That's a bay, right? We hire a boat. I can sit in a boat as well as I can sit in a bed."

He spread his hands. "Fine, we'll do it your way. I tried to help you, and all I managed was to go to the top of ODIN's list of suspects and get threatened with kneecapping."

I nodded with more than a trace of irony. "I really hope I get the chance to feel bad about it and apologize to you. Until then, just make sure we get the flash drive. I repeat, Blakelock, we have no time to waste."

Gallin put her weapon back under her arm and said, "You speak Spanish?"

"Yeah, I speak Spanish."

"You want to get a boat? It needs to be fast and have a cabin and a bunk. We also need a dinghy so we can go ashore."

He arched an eyebrow at her. "You sure you trust me to do that?"

"Cut it out. We can't afford to be prima donnas. You made a mistake. Get it right this time."

I saw his face flush with anger. He stood and left. We waited in silence till we heard the front door close. Then Gallin went down to make sure he'd actually left. A couple of minutes later, she returned and stood in the doorway looking at me.

"What do you think?" she said.

"I don't know. What about you? You've talked to him more than I have."

She shrugged and went to sit with her ass on the windowsill. "My first impression was good. If he was working for the Cabal, or dealing with them, he could have taken us both out at the airport. But he didn't. He went to some trouble to save your life."

"So why the bullshit about not wanting to tell us where the drive was?"

"Maybe he doesn't trust us. There is no reason why he should. He said himself about the only person he trusts is

Nero. Nero trusted him, as much as he trusts anybody. I'm just playing devil's advocate here, but he might be a good guy and these bastards are holding something over him. They have a lot of power and a long reach. All we can do is be on our guard."

I nodded. "OK."

"Are you going to get up?"

"Just as soon as you leave the room, I am."

She snorted. "You ain't got nothin' I ain't seen on my five brothers, boy," she said in what she probably thought was a Texan accent.

"Well, you don't know that, do you, Gallin?"

She arched an eyebrow at me. "I can imagine. You want to tell me how you're going to get dressed with just one arm?"

Over the next five minutes, taking great care to keep her eyes fixed on mine, she dressed me and helped me to make my way downstairs to a large, open-plan living room with sliding glass doors that gave on to a large swimming pool. As she sat me on the sofa, I told her, "I need to talk to your dad."

"Why?"

"Because if Blakelock fails us, Natalya is our last best chance."

"Ivanova? How do you figure that?"

"Get your laptop and connect me. I'll explain as we go."

She went back upstairs and came down a couple of minutes later with her computer. She set it up on the coffee table in front of me and called Gabriel on her cell phone. She spoke to him in Hebrew, and a couple of minutes later, his face appeared on the screen.

"You were shot," he said.

"It could be worse," I told him. "How are things with Dr. Ivanova?"

"She is still here, at the embassy. She is not very cooperative, Alex. She says she will not speak to us until you return. She believes we have assassinated you and will assassinate her at the first opportunity. I told her, 'Opportunity? What better opportunity than now?' But she won't listen."

"Has she said anything to you about an American general?"

"No." He shook his head.

"I need to talk to her. It's beyond urgent, Gabriel. Can you have her brought to you now?"

He reached off screen. I heard him speak. It was partly muttering, then he said, "Tell her Alex Mason wants to see her." He turned back to me and said, "She is on her way. Can you tell me what this is about?"

I thought about it and didn't see any reason why not.

"Do you know anything about General William H. Drake?"

"I have heard the name. I can't say I know much about him, an advisor to several presidents... Why is he important?"

"He is a man with top security clearance. I believe he heard about Dr. Geller's research and contacted him with information. I asked Dr. Ivanova to arrange a meeting with him."

He frowned. "You are still in Menorca?"

"Yes."

"Then if you are making this call as a matter of urgency from there, things have not gone well."

"I don't know, Gabriel. Right now, nothing is clear, and I am trying to cover my bases."

There was a noise in the background. Gabriel stood, and for a moment all I could see was a button on his blue shirt.

Then he moved and that was replaced by Natalya's beautiful, drawn face.

"Alex," she said, "I am so happy to see you. Tell me what is happening. I am so scared. Are you safe?"

"I'm fine, Natalya. Now listen carefully because we have very little time. Did you contact General Drake?"

Her face went like stone. "No."

"I need you to contact him, Natalya. This is beyond urgent. This is a matter of life and death."

"I don't know where he is."

"You told me you could contact him for me. I am depending on you, Natalya. You are my last hope. I am serious."

Her eyes strayed away from the screen in front of her. "David said we were at the end of history. End of days, he said. General Drake told him this."

"I know, Natalya. That is why it is so important that I speak to him."

Her eyes came back to me. "I do not trust these people. How do I know they will not kill me or put me in prison? How do I know?"

"Because they have made a promise to me, and I have made a promise to you. Right now, Natalya, you are more valuable to us than you can imagine. Remember what you asked me in London?"

"What did I ask you, Alex?"

"What does it take for evil to prosper? In this case it takes one good woman to do nothing."

She closed her eyes. "Always so brutal."

"I *need* to talk to him. I need you to arrange a meeting, or tell me how I can contact him."

"I will call him."

"Now, Natalya. Gabriel, can you give her a secure phone?" I heard movement and activity. I said, "Natalya. Tell him I am a friend of David's, that you know you can trust me, and I need to speak to him urgently."

Somebody handed her a phone, and she stood, and for a moment the screen was filled with her blouse. A moment after that, it was replaced by Gabriel's face.

"Who is this general, Alex?"

"Dr. Geller told Dr. Ivanova that General Drake had conclusive proof of the existence of the Cabal and the identity of their principal members. He is himself a senior member. The story is he is secretly opposed to their plans. Dr. Geller suspected that the Cabal had become aware of his association with the general and that was why he feared he was going to be killed and made the flash drive."

Gabriel groaned softly and ran his fingers through his hair. "It is possible then that they have already got to the general and killed him."

"Yes," I said. "Yes, it's possible."

His eyes now strayed away from the screen, and I gathered he was watching Natalya, listening to her speak. After a while he stood, and she sat and stared out of the screen at me again.

"I called his private line, Alex, but his personal secretary answered me. He is gone."

"Gone? What do you mean, gone?"

"Camping."

"*Camping?* In November? Where the hell has he gone camping, in Australia?"

"I asked his secretary where. He said he did not know. The

general told him he needed to get away for a few days. He said he would call."

"But he left his personal phone with his secretary."

She nodded. "Yes. I am sorry. I have failed you."

Gabriel leaned into the picture behind Natalya's shoulder. "He is going to ground, Alex. If this is the case, he has taken his car. He is not flying because he does not want to be on any passenger list. He will not be using credit cards. He will be using cash or a card from a numbered account. Is Aila there? Aila! Aila, are you there?"

Gallin leaned in across me with her elbow on my leg.

"I'm here."

He rattled at her in Hebrew and she occasionally nodded. When he'd finished, she said, "OK" and sat up.

Gabriel continued speaking, to me now.

"Maybe we can help, Alex. We have a lot of experience finding people who do not want to be found. Aila will work with some colleagues on the net. I will have a word with Nero. I will not mention you. Between us, we can find him. I have no doubt General Drake is a very intelligent man, but disappearing is a skill that even expert operatives find very, very difficult these days."

"Thank you, Gabriel. Let's hope we find him before they do."

"We'll be in touch."

Gallin reached over and switched off the screen. Then she turned to me with her face a few inches from mine, and said, "Lie down."

I tried to think of a wiseass answer but felt suddenly too tired.

"I made a chicken stew last night," she said, "I am going to give you a mug of broth, and while you drink broth and recover, me and the boys are going to look for General Drake. Don't argue, or I will poke you in your left pectoral."

"Nice as that sounds," I said, maneuvering myself into a reclining position, "I think I'll just lie here and drink broth."

"Wise choice."

She brought me the mug of broth, richly seasoned with olive oil and black pepper, and I sipped it while she sat with her laptop and worked silently. Pretty soon my eyes grew heavy, and I slipped into unconsciousness.

When I opened them again, the quality of the light had changed. It was more copper than bright, and the shadows in the room had grown longer. Gallin had her computer on her lap, but her chin was in her hand, and she was staring out at the lawn and the pool and the sighing pines.

"Where's Blakelock?" I asked.

"He's not back yet."

I frowned. "How long's he been gone?"

Three hours." She turned to look at me. "He's either been killed, or he's betrayed us."

"Son of a bitch." I levered myself into a painful sitting position. "Cala Lucalari. Was that a lie? A red herring? Or was he telling the truth and they've taken him out?"

"I've been asking myself the same question."

"And there's only one answer. We don't know."

She nodded. "We have to go there. But you're in no shape, Mason."

"I agree. But that's tough shit for me. You can't go alone, and we can't wait for backup. We have to go. We have no choice."

She stared at me for a long moment. Finally she nodded. "Yeah. OK."

"We need to rent a boat."

"I've done that."

"Already?"

"After two hours. I've been sitting here wondering how to stop you from coming."

"Don't do that, Gallin. Some things are more important than that. You can't do this on your own. It's my left arm that's damaged. I can still use a pistol."

"Yeah. I agree. Come on, let's go."

I got to my feet, and she draped my jacket over my shoulders and slipped my Sig into my waistband. We made our way out to the rental. As I climbed with difficulty into the passenger seat, I asked her, "Did you make any progress with the general?"

"I'm not sure. It's tricky." She slammed her door and pulled out of the gate onto the main road to Mahon. "Most people don't realize—even people who should know better—that modern cars all have GPS, which means you can locate them pretty easily. The boys found he was driving a Lexus and got his license plate, and pretty soon we found him driving south through Utah. Then he must have realized his GPS was traceable because his car stopped at a motel near Beaver, on I-15, and vanished."

"Damn. So now what?"

"All is not lost. We checked the gas stations he would have passed and looked for credit card receipts on numbered accounts."

"That's good, and?"

"We found one. They're pretty rare. And this one was used at the motel in Beaver, where his Lexus went off air."

"Does Nero know about this?"

"I'm pretty sure he doesn't."

"Good, let's keep it that way."

"What are you thinking?"

"We go to this cove. It's a hopeless exercise. As he himself said, there is no way we can find it without him, but we have to try. You never know, we might find him there, or the assassin."

"Agreed."

"Assuming we fail, which we probably will, we trace General Drake's credit card and fly to intercept him."

She nodded as we turned onto the ME-2 into the city. "That was what I had thought too. When we get the drive—or the general—Mason, you realize that's when the *real* problems *really* start. That is when the crap hits the fan."

"Yeah, I know."

THIRTEEN

We stopped at the URentaYacht office on Moll de Llevant, which apparently meant 'Quay of the Rising,' reflecting the fact that it was in the east. Gallin went in, signed the papers, paid for the boat, and collected the keys while I stayed in the Jeep, felt sorry for myself, and watched the copper light chop and ripple on the harbor waters.

After ten or fifteen minutes, she came out holding a blue plastic folder. She ran across the road and clambered behind the wheel, dropping the folder on my lap.

"We park up there," she said and pointed through the windshield at the Moll de Ponent, which meant the 'Quay of the Setting' because it was in the west.

"The quay of the Rising Sun and the Quay of the Setting Sun. That's pretty cool, Gallin. I think maybe I should retire and write fantasy novels about the world after the ice caps melt and what's left of humanity begins to re-emerge. What do you think?"

She spoke looking over her shoulder as she pulled out into

the traffic. "I think you're delirious and we need to get you back to DC before you die on me."

"Maybe we could buy a ranch in Wyoming and raise horses and have kids. Or have horses and raise kids."

She ignored me. I didn't blame her because I wasn't making a lot of sense. Some part of me knew it was probably residual shock, but right then I didn't care. Gallin pulled into a space in the parking lot and killed the engine. She studied me a moment. She looked worried, and that made me smile.

"Are you going to be OK to walk?"

"Sure."

"It's not far. Then you can lie down on the bunk."

"OK."

"We're going to cover about twenty miles in the boat. I want to get there soon, but I don't want to draw a lot of attention. So we're going to be doing about ten or twelve knots, OK? We're looking at about two hours."

"I'll be OK, Gallin." I was aware I sounded sleepy when I said it and added, "Let's do this."

She grabbed her laptop from the back of the vehicle, which I thought was odd, and then we set off at a stroll. It was a couple of minutes' walk from the car to the boat. I tried to hide it but I was feeling tired, and my left shoulder was killing me.

The Star of Mahon was a thirty-five foot motor launch in blue and white with a sunbathing deck on the prow and a sitting-eating-drinking deck at the stern. The helm, or steering wheel to land-lubbers, was inside the cabin with its own chair, compass, GPS, radar and radio, all conveniently set beside the table and the seating area.

By the time we had cast off and started pulling away from the quay, Gallin did not need to convince me to stretch out on the couch and crash. I found the first aid box, took four painkillers, and collapsed. After that, the hum of the motors and the steady slap of the small waves against the hull made short work of putting me to sleep.

When I reemerged into consciousness, the sun had sunk behind the horizon, and what had probably been a spectacular blaze of color in the west was now a fading hint of mauve.

I levered myself into a sitting position and rubbed my face with my right hand.

"How long was I out?"

"A little over an hour. Are you feeling any better? You had me a little worried back there."

I smiled. "I still like the idea of retiring to Wyoming and writing fantasy novels," I told her. She arched an eyebrow but didn't look at me. "But I feel better for having slept. Are we alone? Did we pick up a tail?"

She shook her head. "I don't think so. It's hard to tell out here, but I've been keeping a look out, and I haven't seen anything. Nothing on the radar, either." She was quiet for a moment, then, "You think he'll be there?"

"Maybe. It depends how much of a lead he has on us." I thought a moment, then added, "It also depends on where and how he hid the drive. It's unlikely he just dug a hole in the sand and put a rock on it. If he went up in the pinewoods and did something more elaborate, we might just get lucky and intercept him on his way back."

She glanced at me a moment and nodded once. "Yeah, maybe."

I sighed, still feeling tired and suddenly depressed. "But the most likely scenario is we'll find the drive gone and Blakelock dead."

"That is the most likely scenario," she said quietly. "Let's be ready for that." She was silent for a moment. "If that's the case, or he's not there, what do you want to do?"

I thought about it. "I'll tell you what I'd *like* to do. I'd like to systematically take out everyone on that list, except General Drake."

She smiled for the first time since I'd woken up. "You want to do that? We're pretty good at that stuff." After a moment, she added absently, "There are rumors there's an agency that does that..."

I glanced at her, then sighed. "I don't know. Isn't that becoming your enemy? You protect the Rule of Law by executing your enemies without trial."

She snorted. "That's fine for men with pipes and beards, but in the end, it's all subjective. If you are at war and there are men physically invading your land and killing your people, you don't arrest them and put them on trial so a jury of their peers can decide whether they are guilty. You shoot the bastards, you booby-trap their communication systems, you isolate them and you bomb them and you keep hitting them until they stop and desist." After a moment's silence, she added, "I would sooner explain to my daughter why I am in prison than explain to her why I didn't do everything in my power to protect her from being raped and mutilated."

"I'm inclined to agree. But we are not there yet. Let's see what we find at Cala Lucalari."

I dozed fitfully for the next forty-five minutes as dusk turned to night over the dark ocean. After a time, I became aware of a shift in the sound of the engine. The lights went out, we slowed, and I heard the surge and slosh of the water around the bows as we began to turn. I opened my eyes. "Are we there?"

"Yeah," she said quietly. "This is it. I killed the lights. I don't want to be seen."

I climbed out onto the deck and made my way forward, where I lay and scanned the shore and the water. The cala was like a small, Mediterranean fjord, maybe a hundred and fifty feet across, with tall, craggy rock cliffs on either side and a rocky beach at the end where the land rose steadily toward a wooded sierra.

There was no moon, and in the lea of the cliffs the shadows were almost impenetrable, but as we crept forward by starlight, I began to see a glint to my left, close to the shore. At first I thought it was the luminous foam from the small, sighing waves. But pretty soon I realized it was the hull of a launch similar to our own, rocking gently at anchor.

I looked back painfully over my shoulder. I couldn't see Gallin, but I knew she could see me. I held up my palm, then pointed toward the boat. She killed the engine, letting the boat drift gently toward the shore some fifty yards away. A moment later, she dropped on her belly beside me. I pointed and spoke softly.

"There's a boat anchored just off the beach. If it was just tourists, they'd have a light burning, so it seems likely it's Blakelock."

"I see it."

"I can't see another one. So either Blakelock came alone and is possibly still here..."

"Or his killer came, found him, killed him, and left."

"Or he was brought here against his will."

"Right. We're pretty much where we were, except that now we know he's here somewhere."

I nodded. We remained like that for maybe five minutes, allowing our eyes to become accustomed to the dark, searching for movement, glints or glimmers, but there was nothing, just the gentle rock and sigh of the water and the soft, luminous glow of the surf on the sand. Eventually she whispered close to my ear, "You going to be OK in the dinghy?"

"Yeah, let's do it."

"I'll get a flashlight."

It was a gray inflatable with paddles. We clambered in from the boarding platform at the stern of the yacht, and Gallin rowed us the fifty yards to the beach, where the small waves carried us the last few feet onto the sand. There we jumped out, and between us—I one-handed—we dragged the dinghy out of the water and into the shelter of the rocks. There we both hunkered down and listened, scanning the darkness among the sparse pinewoods on the slope, the stony beach, and the cliffs.

Gallin breathed, "Not a damned thing."

I pointed along the sighing shore. "Let's walk. He might be lying there, dead."

We stood. I took the shoreline, where the water splashed and rolled around my feet. Gallin walked parallel, about fifteen feet farther in, looking for any kind of man-sized object, darker than the darkness. There was nothing other than rocks and driftwood.

It was when we were maybe twenty yards from the far cliff that I raised my eyes and stopped. I spoke softly. "Gallin."

She stopped and looked back at me. I could barely make out her features in the pale starlight. I pointed at the cliff face, just fifty or sixty feet from us, directly ahead. There was an oblong some seven feet high and three or four feet across.

"A door?"

"A door in the cliff face."

I pulled my weapon and saw her do the same. I took two long steps out of the water so my feet would make no noise, and we approached, one on either side of the door. She flattened herself against the cliff face and pulled the flashlight from her belt. Our eyes met. She gave me the nod and flipped on the powerful beam. I swung around, dropped to one knee, and aimed where the beam struck.

It struck Blakelock. He was sitting on a straight-backed chair. Heavy duty tape bound his legs, his arms, and his body to it, and there was tape over his mouth. His face was badly bruised, and his eyes were closed.

I stepped in, and Gallin followed, playing the beam around us. It was a strange place. It was like an artificial, room-shaped cave carved out of the living rock. Aside from a few rocks and sand, there was nothing inside the place besides Blakelock.

I approached him, and Gallin shone the light on him. I felt his throat for a pulse.

"He's alive."

I holstered my weapon and pulled my penknife from my pocket. I cut through the tape, and he sagged forward. She said, "If he's alive, whoever did this to him is coming back."

I looked up at her. It made sense. The only reason they wouldn't have killed him would be because they were checking out whatever he had told them about where he'd put the drive. She said, "We have to get him to the dinghy before they get back." But even as she was saying it, I could see she knew she was wrong.

I said, "What if he told them the truth, and they have the drive?"

"Then we have to wait for them."

We both looked at Blakelock. We shared the unspoken thought that we didn't know how badly hurt he was, that he might die if we didn't get him help. But the consequences of not recovering the drive were unthinkable.

First it was a change in his breathing, a kind of spluttering and coughing. Then he raised his head. I hunkered down beside him. His voice was barely a whisper.

"*Mason...*"

"Yeah, we're here."

"*You have to...*"

Gallin approached and hunkered down in front of him. "How many are there, Peter?"

"*You have to... He's...*"

"Just one?"

"*In the cave...*"

I said, "In the cove? Where did you send him, Blakelock? Did you tell him where it was?"

"*In the cave. He hurt me a lot, Mason.*" He began to weep. "*He hurt me a lot...*"

I'll never really know why we didn't see it. When you shine a bright light in a dark place, the dark bits outside the beam get darker. Maybe that was the reason. I have tried to replay it in my mind a hundred times, and I think maybe Gallin's flashlight cast Blakelock's shadow long and black across the opening in the corner, but the fact is that we never saw the entrance to the cave. The room they had carved in the face of the cliff was the antechamber. I was later told it was a smuggler's cave. That may well be. The fact is it ran from that room all the way up through the cliff and came out above, concealed among dense ferns and pine trees. That was where Blakelock had hidden the drive, and that was where he had sent his interrogator.

The flash was blinding, and the noise in that confined space was deafening. The top of Blakelock's head erupted in a black spray that was visible for just a second. I reacted automatically and hurled myself at Gallin, knocking her on her back, wrenching the flashlight from her hand and hurling it across the room. The flash exploded again three times, giving me the shooter's location. I rolled away from Gallin with pain searing through my left shoulder, and on his third shot, I returned fire. I heard a violent cuss, and then there was a large, black figure moving, running across the room.

I trained my gun on the luminous oblong of the door. Gallin had obviously had the same thought because when the hulking figure obscured the door, we both rained fire on him.

He ducked and cried out in pain but kept running. Gallin ran for her flashlight, and I went after him. When I got through the door, I could see no sign of him. I hunkered down so as not to make a target and snapped at Gallin over my shoulder, "Keep down! I don't see him!"

She crawled out on her belly. Below us and to the right, I could hear sounds. A soft splash, a ripple, and then he came into sight. He was in a dinghy like ours, rowing out toward the boat.

She said, "If he makes the boat we're lost. If we sink the dinghy, he'll still make the boat swimming. It's too close."

I stood and took aim one-handed. I fired one shot. The Sig spat fire, and the crack echoed around the cove. He stopped rowing. Very slowly he leaned over to the side, rolled, and fell with a loud splash into the water.

I was suddenly aware that Gallin had pulled off her boots and was running down toward the beach. She crashed in, kicking up luminous foam, and dove. It wasn't far to where the dinghy was sitting, bobbing on the small waves, just twenty or thirty feet. When she got there, she went under.

Anxiety twisted in my gut, and I made my way to the waterline, trying hard to ignore the pain in my arm and the warm trickle of blood from the torn stitches. I was ankle deep by the time her head burst from the black water. She took a deep breath and went down again. She did that twice more, but the third time she held up her hand and began to swim back, still holding her hand above her head. Soon she was standing, sodden and dripping water, wading out onto the rocky shore. In her hand, she had the drive and held it up for me to see.

"You are one shit-hot shot, big guy. You're a very fine marksman. You hit him right in the heart."

I took the shattered remains of the steel pen drive and looked at them in my palm.

"What a shame," she said, "that he'd put it in his left breast pocket."

FOURTEEN

Back on the boat, she said, "You up to taking us home?"

"Sure. If I fall asleep, just kick me."

"Don't tempt me," she said but smiled. She set herself up at the table with her laptop, and I turned us around one-handed and set the course back to Mahon. We didn't talk except that once or twice I was about to nod off and she barked at me, then grinned. As we came into port, she closed up her computer and slipped it back in her bag. Then she came over, used her hips and ass to move me away from the helm, and took us into dock. When we were done, she came and punched me gently on the chest.

"Come on, hot shot. You've earned some of Mama Gallin's chicken broth and a good rest. Let's get you home."

She returned the keys to the rental company, and we drove back to the villa in silence. Once there, she set me up on the sofa, removed my shoes and my socks, gave me a couple of powerful pain killers and a large mug of chicken stew, and settled herself at the table with her laptop again. I had been putting on a brave face, but the truth was I was in a lot of pain and I was exhausted. So before very long, I was drifting toward the Land of Nod.

"You're a strange woman," I told her as I drifted.

"That's what the surgeon told my mother," she said absently, "when he was removing my tail and the little horns."

"Complex and contradictory," I said and slipped into a deep, soothing ocean. At first it felt peaceful and restful, but after a while, I began to notice shadows, the giant shadows of giant, faceless killers.

A voice said to me, "OK, big guy. Time to wake up." I opened my eyes. She pointed at the table beside me and said, "Drink your broth."

"I only just got to sleep."

"You've been snoring for an hour and fifteen minutes."

I winced. "I hurt."

"Cowboy up. I have something."

"They can treat that these days."

"I have General Drake's financials for the last year. Obviously he has all the usual stuff, mortgages, repayments on two cars, schools for the kids, electricity, gas, telephone, Wi-Fi, ATM cash withdrawals, et cetera.

"So I have gone through all this shit to see what his patterns are. How often does he go to the ATM? Typically how much does he withdraw? How often does he have larger than normal expenses? How often do they go away for a trip or a holiday?"

"OK, I get the idea. The standard stuff."

"Right, but especially, how often does he use the card on his numbered account."

"And?"

"He doesn't. He just doesn't use it. Until last week, when we saw that he took his car and disappeared and started using that card. It looks like he might have been keeping that card and that account for this kind of eventuality. Part of an emergency pack."

"Huh." I frowned. "What about his family?"

"I had a couple go around to their house to give them the good news that Jesus had come to save them. Just in case, in the last two thousand years, they hadn't got the memo. The house is empty. No one's at home. Maybe Jesus turned up and saved them. More likely they had some kind of fixed protocol. He went one way, she and the kids went to see her parents and were abducted by ET along the way. However they did it, they all disappeared."

"So do you know where he is now?"

She put her head on one side and made a 'See, that's the thing' kind of face and said, "See, Mason, that's the thing. Quite unexpectedly, the Arizona Department of Public Safety reported that General Drake, his wife, and his two kids were killed in a car accident yesterday. Apparently they were driving from Utah to Nevada along the Veterans Memorial Highway, that's I-15, and they crashed at the Virgin River Gorge bridge. The car went over the barrier, dropped something like a hundred and fifty feet, and exploded. The four of them were burnt beyond recognition. Of course the Arizona Department of Public Safety did not know that General Drake and his family had gone missing."

I screwed up my brain and tried to extract some sense from it. "That is not an easy stunt to pull off. For a start you need a morgue that's willing to give you four bodies. Then you need to make the car crash on a busy highway with all the seats occupied by dead people."

She shrugged. "There are two things about this, Mason, that make it interesting. The first is that a couple of witnesses claim they saw a dark sports sedan pass the general's Lexus and a hand reach out and open fire. It was real quick and hard to be sure, but that is what they thought they saw.

"That's one thing. Another thing is that the general's card, the one attached to his numbered account, was used yesterday."

"Before the accident?"

"After, but that's not the best thing. The best thing is that it was used in Tel Aviv and then in the tiny kibbutz village of Sde Boker, where Ben Gurion retired and spent the last twenty years of his life."

"Holy cow."

"Yeah, that's what I said when I read it." She gave me a blank smile. "Kind of, almost. Mine was more colorful."

I sat up. "We take the company plane, but we don't need to trouble Nero just yet. I think we want to surprise him with the good news after we've spoken to General Drake."

"Agreed. I've spoken to the kibbutz security coordinator. He's going to check if they are at the hotel or whether they are actually in the kibbutz."

"Good work. Speaking of hotels, you want to book a room? I'll go and wash my face and pack, one-handed."

She muttered something offensive about my lack of manliness as she sat and rattled at the keys of her laptop.

As I made my way to the shower and stood under the hot stream of water, I thought about the wisdom of taking the company jet. I was genuinely worried. If Nero found out we were headed for Tel Aviv, he would want to know why. And if we told him Blakelock was dead, I had killed his assassin—who might have given us invaluable information—and, not only that but the slug that had killed him, that I had fired, had also annihilated the priceless drive he had sent us to recover—if I told him all that—he might just take us off the case. I know I would.

But on the other hand, booking a regular flight would mean going back four hundred miles west to Madrid, changing planes, flying two thousand two hundred miles east to Tel Aviv and then getting another, local flight over eighty miles south to Sde Boker. With check-in times and time wasted hanging around waiting for boarding onto connecting flights, drinking coffee and perusing books and newspapers, it could take us close on twenty-four hours to travel a distance we could cover in three hours on the company Gulfstream.

But the bottom line, I decided as I rinsed off the lather, was that we needed to be in Sde Boker now, not tomorrow or the day after; and if Nero called to find out what the hell was going on, I'd crackle down the phone at him and make noises about poor signal.

The bathroom door opened after I had finished drying my hair and was trying to pull on my jeans one-handed. Gallin looked at me, sighed, and hauled them up as I said, "Ghghcrck-ghcrackle... poor... ghcrcklck... desert... clkckghghcklckrck... no signal... ghcklrckgh..."

She zipped up my pants and buckled my belt while she stared at me and fought to stifle a laugh. "What the hell are you talking about, Mason?"

"I'm practicing what I am going to tell Nero if he calls for an update."

She nodded in reluctant recognition of my wisdom, helped me finish dressing, and we headed for the airport outside Mahon, where the company jet was waiting.

It was a three-hour flight. I slept most of the way and was awakened when we arrived by the thud and squeal of the landing gear as we touched down in the Negev desert, eighty miles south of Tel Aviv. I checked my watch and saw we were closing on six a.m. Outside, light was dispelling the darkness in the east, turning it blue-gray. I stared. The only way to describe that vast gray, craggy wilderness is to say that it was ancient and biblical. It was a place quintessentially designed for striding along empty, sandy roads wearing sandals and robes and carrying a big staff. It was a place designed by angry, jealous gods to test the human spirit and invariably find it wanting. It was the land of the Elohim.

"How much," I said mainly to myself, "do landscapes shape cultures?"

I heard Gallin give a rueful laugh. "I've spent my whole life wondering that same thing."

I smiled at her. "You live in Wyoming, or even Arizona or New Mexico, and the landscape demands you talk to eagles and badgers, ride horses, and commune with the land. You're born in Scandinavia or Britain, and the landscape demands you grow a beard, grab an axe, take to the sea, and conquer the world. But here, you just have to wear sandals, carry a staff, and have a burning bush talk to you up on a mountain."

"Yup," she said quietly. "And two gets you twenty He'll be talking to you about war, punishment, and vengeance." She gave a small laugh. "See? Tolstoy was Russian. If he'd been Jewish, *War and Peace* would have been three times as long, and he would have called it *War, Punishment, and Vengeance,* with the tagline, 'The Messiah Will Give Us Peace—When He Gets Here.'"

"Wow."

"Yeah, being God's chosen people ain't all that much fun. Ask Woody Allen."

I watched her stand and asked her, "Did you rent a car?"

"Yeah, I got a Grenadier delivered to the airport. They're nice cars, what Land Rover used to be. Tough, this one puts out almost three hundred horses and will do zero to sixty in eight seconds. Not bad for a truck."

"Oh." I had a sinking feeling as I stood, which is counterintuitive when you think about it, but Gallin driving a Toyota Camry is scary. Gallin driving a military four-by-four with three hundred horses under the hood in a biblical desert in Israel defied imagination. "That's good," I lied. "Want me to drive? You must be tired."

She glanced at me like I was insane. "With your arm? Besides, I've been looking forward to putting this baby through its paces. C'mon. You'll love it."

I didn't love it, but I made a brave show of nonchalance as we streaked along a nameless dirt road trailing two miles of dust behind us, with our faces flattened and wobbling like rocket propelled Jell-O. We fishtailed onto Route 204, surged sickeningly onto Highway 40, fishtailed again onto Winery Road, and cruised gently down a series of dusty streets shaded by a wide variety of trees including tall, swaying palm trees and whispering pines, while Gallin smiled.

"Man, I needed that," she said.

We pulled up outside a house with a big lawn and many trees. The shade was a welcome relief from the intense glare of the desert sun.

"This is where they are at, according to the security coordinator."

"Let's go have a chat."

I climbed out with difficulty, and we followed the crazy paving through the shade to the front door. Gallin knocked, then rang the bell.

The door was opened by an attractive woman in her late forties. She managed to smile and frown at the same time, looking first at Gallin and then at me.

"Yes?" she said. The accent was Midwest.

I said, "Mrs. Drake?"

"No." She lost some of the smile. "I'm afraid you've made a mistake. There is no one of that name here."

Gallin delivered the question as smooth as if she'd greased it. "What name do you go by now?"

"Hirsch—" It was out before she could stop it. She closed her eyes and spoke with slow emphasis. "Our name is, and always has been, Hirschfield."

The phrasing was awkward and unnatural, and her face said she could hear herself and knew it. I smiled.

"You had the same name as your husband even before you were married? That must be rare."

"I'm sorry. You have the wrong—"

"No." I cut her short. "We have the right house, Mrs. Hirschfield. Please tell the general we need to talk to him. Please tell him we were friends of David Geller and Yasha Orlev." She hesitated. I said, "We know about the accident in Arizona, we know about the numbered account. We don't care, and we are not interested in any of that. But we do need to talk to the general, urgently."

She was about to deny it all and slam the door in our faces, but I took a small step forward. "We are friends, Mrs. Hirschfield. The people you are afraid of would not bother confirming who you are, believe me. They would kill you on the off chance that you might be the Drake family. And believe me, if we were able to track you this easily, they will be too. If they suspect that the car crash was a setup, they'll start looking, and they'll spot the card. We are risking our careers and our lives by just standing here. We need to talk to the general, and he needs to talk to us."

She stared at us, paralyzed by doubt. Gallin said quietly, "We are *all* at risk as long as we stand here, Mrs. Drake."

Her face twisted with anger and grief. She fought to control it, but it was too much, and she blurted, "We came here to get away from all that! And now you show up!"

Gallin turned and scanned the area while I stepped up and took the general's wife by the shoulders and spoke quietly. "I know. We are here to help. Let's go inside."

I pushed gently, and Gallin came in behind me and closed the door. Mrs. Drake turned away from me and led us into a large, basic living room. The furniture was old and looked like it had been picked up from thrift shops. She took three sudden, hurried steps and turned holding her fists up by her temples, like she was warding off punches to her head.

"I need you to leave," she said. "I can't do this. I need you to leave now. *Now!*"

Gallin came up beside me, speaking quietly, with the kind of authority that only comes from being an active officer on the front line of a conflict zone.

"We are not going to leave, Mrs. Drake. You can call the security coordinator, but I think if you give it a moment's thought, you'll realize you really don't want to do that. Where are your kids?"

Mrs. Drake froze. She stared at Gallin with wide, terrified eyes. Gallin said, "Upstairs. I thought so." She sat on a wooden armchair with green, synthetic fiber upholstery. I sat on a couch of the same 1950s design, and as Mrs. Drake sat on another two-seater, Gallin pointed at me.

"This is Alex Mason. He works for American Intelligence. I am Captain Aila Gallin, I work for the Mossad. You see his arm is in a sling? That's because he was shot just a couple of days ago. He should be in hospital, but what we are doing—the reason we need to see the general—is so important that he has come here with me instead."

She paused a moment, gazing at the floor, pursing her lips and nodding, like she was listening to some internal dialogue.

"Now, Mrs. Drake, I am going to explain something to you. Last night, with his arm in a sling and bleeding from his wound, Mr. Mason shot a professional, international assassin and killed him."

Mrs. Drake gave a small gasp and sat up, staring at me. Gallin went on.

"Me? I am not just an officer in the Mossad. I first became a captain in the IDF. I have seen intense action, and I have killed men on a number of occasions. Now I want you to think about this. If we were here to hurt you or extract information from you, do you really think we'd be here taking all this time and trouble to pacify and relax you? There are quicker and easier ways to get information. But we"—she pointed back and forth from me to her and back again—"we don't do that kind of thing. And we try to stop other people doing that kind of thing. We are what you might call the good guys, and we are here to help you." She paused again and gave a humorless smile. "And believe me, you need help." And as though to drive it home, she leaned forward with her elbows on her knees and said, "If you are alive right now and safe in your home, it is because we mean you no harm. Do you understand that?"

Her gaze drifted to a door behind me. I said, "We know your kids are upstairs, Mrs. Drake. And that is exactly where they are going to stay. Absolutely no harm is going to come to you or your family from us. We are here to help you. You need to take that onboard and accept it, because we are very, very short of time."

FIFTEEN

She sat for a long time with her eyes closed and her hands clasped between her knees. Finally she took a deep breath and opened her eyes.

"I suppose it makes no difference really whether I believe you or not." She hesitated a moment, then nodded like she was agreeing with the voice in her head. "But what you say makes sense. What do you want to know?"

I said, "Where is the general?"

She seemed to turn gray. For a moment, it was as though she had aged ten years. "I honestly don't know."

Gallin said, "You're going to have to explain that."

"We have been here for a few days, almost a week. The crash in Arizona was engineered by some Israeli friends of my husband's. In exchange, they wanted him to come to Israel and talk to some people. Yesterday morning, he told me he was going for a meeting with them. I haven't heard from him since."

I glanced at Gallin and knew she was wondering the same

as me. How come ODIN and the Mossad were cooperating in trying to get hold of the drive, but at the same time the Mossad were trying to get hold of General Drake without telling either Nero, Gabriel, or Gallin?

I turned to Mrs. Drake. "How much do you know about what your husband was involved in?"

She pressed her lips together, and tears welled in her eyes. "Practically nothing. I know he was involved in aspects of intelligence, but he was very secretive and very loyal. He never told me anything at all. This has just come as such a shock."

"Did you know he'd been speaking to Professor David Geller and Dr. Yasha Orlev?"

She was quiet so long I began to think she wasn't going to answer. Eventually she took a deep breath and said, "Yes. He never told me what the conversations were about, but on one occasion he said he was helping them with research that was..." She trailed off, thinking. "It seemed a little mad at the time. He said it would be the most important revelation for mankind since the birth of Sumer."

I frowned. "The birth of who?"

Gallin's voice was quiet and steady and had a quality to it I had never heard before.

"Sumer," she said. "Not who, where. Sumer is where it all began, the whole bloody mess."

My frown deepened. "Sumer, as in the Sumerians? The guys with wristwatches and handbags?"

Gallin's eyes told me she thought I was inappropriate and also not funny. I ignored her and shook my head at Mrs. Drake.

"What has Sumer got to do with Professor Geller's research?"

"I honestly have no idea. All he told me was that their research would be the biggest revelation since that civilization."

Gallin said, half to herself, "The cradle of civilization, at least seven thousand years ago. What the hell were they doing?" Then to Mrs. Drake, "Did your husband keep any notes or any record of his meetings?"

"I think so." She glanced up at the ceiling. "He'd chosen a room upstairs as his den. It's all a jumble of boxes at the moment. If you want to look…"

I caught Gallin's eye, and she understood. She stayed talking to the general's wife while I climbed the stairs and stood at the open door of the room that had obviously been intended as his den. There was a plain pine desk up against the far wall, stacked high with cartons full of papers, files, and notebooks. In the corner there was a green steel filing cabinet with three drawers. A black leather chair with wheels stood at an angle to the desk and was also stacked with papers and notebooks. Six more cartons stood on the floor, brimming with everything from desk lamps and staplers to paperweights, photographs, and crumpled magazines.

I fought off a creeping feeling of helplessness. What was I looking for? A clue. A clue to where he might be. A clue that might not even be here, and if it was, where the hell did I begin to look?

I spent ten, maybe fifteen minutes looking through boxes and flicking through notes in notebooks. I found nothing of any interest. Most of it looked like some pretty tame memoirs he seemed to be working on. There was nothing that suggested any place he might have gone, either to contact someone or to seek refuge.

I wondered if he had simply gone to Tel Aviv and been

taken in by the Mossad. But then why not tell Gabriel and Gallin?

Hell, why not tell Nero?

I sat on a hardback chair, and while I turned the problem over in my mind, some other part continued to observe the room. And it struck me that the only piece of furniture that had actually been placed—put where it was meant to be—was a framed map of Israel. Like he'd wanted to study it.

The couple of times I had moved into a new home, the first thing I had placed had always been the beer in the fridge and then my desk and my computer. From what I could see, the desk was laden with everything that wasn't on the floor, and not even his chair had been put in place. As for his computer, it was in pieces among all the other junk. But the map of Israel was there, hanging on the wall.

I stood, moved to the map, and scanned it minutely. There was a spot. You wouldn't notice it unless you were looking for it. It had been circled in pencil, and then the pencil rubbed out. Thirty-five miles north and a little east of Sde Boker and twenty-four miles west of the Dead Sea: a big, bare mountain, like a giant pyramid in the middle of the Yatir Forest, right on the Israel National Trail.

Drake. You couldn't get much more English than Drake.

I went halfway down the stairs and leaned on the banisters. Gallin and Mrs. Drake turned to look at me.

"Mrs. Drake, is your husband Jewish?"

She shook her head. "No. He is very sympathetic to Israel and her predicament, but he always says that the Abrahamic religions are barbaric and primitive. His parents were both Methodists. Both sides of his family were originally from England, before the Declaration of Independence. They were

Anglicans, then became Methodists. But he himself had been an atheist all his adult life. He was rather bitter about it." She gave a smile that had more of sadness than humor about it. "It was as though he felt God had betrayed him, betrayed us all."

I sighed, wondering if panic was sending me off on a wild goose chase, and finished my descent of the stairs. As I approached them, I asked her, "Did he have any interest in philosophy? Had he recently acquired an interest in philosophy? Had he been trying to find some kind of meaning or reason to things?"

She listened with care, frowning at me. "How could you know that?" she asked.

"Just a hunch. Is that right? Had he?"

"Yes, for the last couple of years, he had become increasingly interested in Zen. He said it was like existentialism without all the depression and heavy drinking and chain smoking."

"This is just a hunch, Mrs. Drake. I just have one more question for you." I saw Gallin's eyebrows arch high but ignored her. "Was this interest in Zen accompanied by an interest in the Samurai?"

Even as I asked it, my eyes had strayed to the three volumes on the bookcase against the wall: *Budo the Way of War*, *Zen and the Art of the Samurai*, and *Zen Budo*.

She followed my gaze and spoke very quietly. "He had become practically obsessed with it."

"And that was what prompted him to contact Professor Geller."

"I had that impression, yes."

I looked at Gallin. "We need to go. Call your office and get them to put a guard on this house. Better still"—I looked at

Mrs. Drake—"have them take Mrs. Drake and her kids into protective custody for the next week."

She nodded and stepped out of the room, pulling her cell from her pocket. I turned back to the general's wife.

"Mrs. Drake, I have only a couple more questions for you, but your answers could be extremely important, so I want you to think very carefully and try to be as accurate as you can. You need to be aware that this investigation could go well beyond any attempt on you and your husband's lives. Do you understand that?"

She looked at me a moment before answering. Then she nodded and said, "Yes. I am beginning to understand that."

"Think very carefully. There is no right answer, OK? Did your husband ever mention the Yatir Forest to you?"

Her gaze became abstracted. After a moment, she said, "Yes. I can't remember in what context. I think he said it was an extraordinary achievement. I think it has over four million trees, and a great variety, despite being in the desert. He was increasingly into nature and conservation as he got older. He said he'd like to visit the place." Her brow contracted, and she seemed to squint. "Why? What relevance..." She trailed off.

I made an effort to smile and gave a meaningless nod.

"Sometimes in investigation it's a case of grasping as many straws as you can and hope that one of them gives you something."

She didn't look very impressed. Gallin came in slipping her phone in her back pocket.

"The security coordinator is going to put a couple of guys outside your house, Mrs. Drake. Meanwhile, somebody is going to come and pick you up and take you and your kids somewhere safe. We are going to go and look for your husband and see if we can bring him home for you."

I hesitated a moment. "And Mrs. Drake, if anybody asks you about our visit, we asked if you knew where the general was, you said you didn't, and we left. We don't know yet who his friends are. So let's play this as close to our chest as we can for now."

She nodded, and we showed ourselves out.

The sun was rising toward the midheaven, glaring down on the desiccated land, and the sky was white, tinted with blue at the edges. It was hot, and the air was motionless.

Gallin swung in behind the wheel of the beast, and I clambered in one-handed, trying to make it look easy. She fired up the big beast and asked, "You feel like telling me what you found?"

I scratched my head and said, "Yeah..." wondering if I knew myself.

"Where are we going?"

"North. Take the 204 north across the desert as far as Dimona, and I'll tell you what I found and how I interpret it."

She made a face that was a little skeptical but said she was giving me the benefit of the doubt.

"OK, what do I do when we get to Dimona?"

"You take Highway 25 north as far as Be'er Aro'er, and then follow Highway 80 all the way to Beit Yatir."

She was already driving, heading out of town. She said, "The forest? You think he's hiding in the forest?"

"No, but I think he got philosophy. Other people get religion, but he is too hard-nosed and pragmatic for that. So he got philosophy, and most precisely, he got Budo."

"The Japanese way of war."

"As I am sure you know, it was quite common among the Samurai. After a life of extreme violence and bloodshed, they would withdraw to a temple and end their days in meditation and contemplation."

"That's true."

"Well, I am not sure if you are aware of it, Gallin, but on the western extreme of the forest, there is a very high, steep hill, rather like a pyramid, which is almost completely bare of trees. It has a flat top, and built right on that flat surface is a small Zen monastery. I think he's gone there."

"I saw the books, but that's not a lot to go on."

"Yeah, I know." I clung to my seat as she squealed onto the 204 and floored the pedal. "But he had a map on his wall in the study, and he had marked the temple in pencil, then rubbed it out. That, with his sudden disappearance and the recent interest in Zen, I suspect he knew that crossing the Cabal would cost him his life, and he wanted to draw fire away from his wife and kids, and at the same time make some kind of peace in his soul."

"Why here? Why Israel?"

I shrugged. "Because this is where it hits the fan, and because he knows that Israel would oppose a collective, global dystopia. He knows that the Mossad will help him in exchange for what he knows. Perhaps he plans to meet them at the monastery."

She was frowning. "What makes you say Israel would oppose a global dystopia, assuming it's true such a thing is being engineered?"

I was surprised and let my face say so. "Are you serious? I would say it's built into your DNA. The history of the Jewish people is defined by one dystopia after another persecuting or exploiting them. Or trying to."

She didn't answer, and we drove on in silence through that harsh, bare landscape. Eventually we came to a town called Yeruham, where they had somehow managed to coax a lush forest park from the dead, yellow sand around a lake. Here she came off at the circle and followed the road down through the shade of the trees to the water's edge. She parked in the dappled shade of a copse and swung down from the cab. I followed her through the dry dust onto a wooden pier that reached out into the water, where great patches of rushes and reeds reached up toward the white-blue sky.

She pulled off her boots and sat with her feet over the edge, lapped by the small waves. I sat beside her, though I kept my shoes on.

"I am not religious, Mason. If there is a god, it knows I'm fallible because it made me that way. What I believe in is my family, I believe in my countries"—she glanced at me—"England and Israel, and I believe in the Jewish culture. They are all things I know. But I can't believe in something I don't know. I believe faith should come from knowledge. Knowledge cannot come from faith. That way madness lies."

I nodded. "Sure, I agree."

"But there are weird things in the Jewish Bible."

I frowned. "Yeah? Like what?"

"Lots, but right now, from the Nevi'im, that's the book of prophets, Ezekiel 38." I raised my eyebrows and my shoulders an eighth of an inch and shook my head. She sighed. "I'm paraphrasing, but basically it says that a prince whom he calls Gog will unite Iran and Russia, along with Central Asia, Turkey,

Sudan, and Libya, for the purpose of sacking and destroying Israel. They will all be led by a man called Gog."

She gazed down at the water and sighed, making small splashing motions with her feet.

"I have no time for conspiracy theories. There's enough crazy shit going down in the world without conspiracy theories. But in all these centuries, it has seemed so unlikely that Russia, Iran, and Central Asia should ever unite and march on Israel. Yet now, out of the blue, Russia, with North Korea, is suddenly an ally of Iran, and Iran's proxies are hurling rockets over our northern border. Just how close are we to Ezekiel 38?"

"We can't think that way, Gallin. If we start thinking in terms of fate and prophecy, we are screwed."

She watched me but seemed not to hear me. "Do you know what Gog means?"

"No."

"It means Roof."

"Roof?"

"The guy who engineers this attack on Israel is called Roof."

"There you go. It doesn't make a lot of sense, does it?"

"Do you know what Vladimir Putin means?"

"Don't tell me it means roof because I won't believe you."

"A rough translation would be Ruler of the World." She held my eye for a long moment. "Would you say that makes him the tops...?"

SIXTEEN

I punched her gently on the shoulder with my left hand.

"Hey, you cannot base your decisions today on the writings of a man who lived two thousand six hundred years ago. We don't know if he was being visited by aliens, talking to God, or eating magic mushrooms! I am not being disrespectful, Gallin. At least I don't mean to be, but we need urgently to find General William Drake, now, today, in 2024, and we cannot go chasing wild geese across Babylon and Palestine seeking deep, biblical meanings to things."

She didn't say anything. She lifted her feet out of the water and pulled on her socks and her boots. She stood, and I stood with her.

"Don't be mad at me, Gallin. We haven't got time to be mad at each other. We have to stay focused."

She put her finger on my chest and stared at my button. "What are the chances, Mason, that two thousand six hundred years ago, a Jewish priest would see an alliance between Persia and Russia at the end of times?"

"OK, granted—"

"And have we ever—even during the Cuban missile crisis—have we *ever* been closer to a manmade extinction event?"

"No."

"So do me just one favor, will you? Keep that Anglo-Saxon mind of yours open."

"Agreed. It's open. It's just in a hurry. Now can we go and look for Drake?"

But as she turned the key and fired up the big engine and we pulled away, headed back toward the 204, I couldn't shake a feeling she had planted in my mind. And she herself put it into words a moment later.

"Cabal," she said, "and let me remind you, Alex Mason, that I am at best an agnostic. I am not a religious person, despite being a Jew from the soles of my feet to the top of my head. Cabal, the word cabal, comes from a Hebrew word, Kabbalah, which means received wisdom."

She glanced at me and shrugged. "Received from where? God? Like the Koran?" She shook her head. "Uh-uh. Received from the elders." She wagged a finger at me, keeping her eyes on the road. "The Kabbala's earliest roots are in Merkava mysticism. Ever heard of it?" I shook my head. "I didn't think so. Not many people have. It appeared in Palestine in the first century after Christ. Its main focus was—and get this, Mr. Anglo-Empirical-Saxon—on the ecstatic and mystical contemplation of the divine throne. Do you know what the divine throne is?"

"No, but I am pretty sure I will in about two minutes or less."

"The divine throne is a chariot—the *Merkava*, the chariot seen in a vision by none other than the prophet Ezekiel himself. You know the one where he saw a windstorm coming out of the north and a cloud with flashing lightning, and in the center it was like glowing metal, and there were four beings who looked human, but they had four faces and four wings?"

"I know the one, Gallin. What's your point?"

"That in chapter thirty-eight of that very text, Ezekiel says that God told him that Gog, the chief prince of Rosh, would lead many nations, including Iran, to attack Israel."

"We already talked about that, Gallin. You have to let it go."

"Maybe *I* have to let it go, Mason, but this group we are up against, the Cabal, how big a part does all this stuff play in what motivates them? Is it a pure coincidence that Drake fled to Israel? Is it pure coincidence that Russia's ally, Iran, is an Islamic dystopia that draws its laws from *the same books* as the Jews? Is it a coincidence that Ezekiel is a prophet recognized by Islam?"

"Gallin, stop! You are doing my head in. What are you saying? What is your point?"

She took a deep breath and closed her eyes, which was alarming because we were cruising at a hundred miles per hour. She opened them again and said, "You are telling me I need to let go of the wild geese that could lead us on a time-wasting romp through ancient Abrahamic lore."

"Nicely put."

"I am saying to you that those Abrahamic texts and the philosophies that flowed from them, the Torah, the Kabbalah, the *Sefer Yetzira*, the early Jewish texts on magic and cosmology, might actually *be* the philosophical core, the philosophical base, of the Cabal. It could be what is motivating them, and *that* is why the prophecy seems to be materializing."

I thought about what she was saying, and a coldness seemed to settle on my skin. A note in one of the general's pads sprang to my mind: *etymology of cipher, sefirot, the ten divine numbers of God the Creator, plus the twenty-two letters of the Hebrew alphabet. Together they form the number of the Illuminati, thirty-two, and constitute the thirty-two paths of secret wisdom.*

"Jesus Christ, Gallin. This is all we needed. It just sounds completely crazy. Are you sure about this?"

I looked at her. She was staring fixedly out through the windshield.

"No," she said. And then, "Yes."

I turned away, stared out of the side window, and whispered, "*Shit!*" with real feeling.

After a while, she said, "It doesn't change things. It doesn't change anything. You're right. You're right! It just gives us a possible insight into who they are and what they are about."

"Right," I said and tried to sound like I meant it. I failed.

It was only sixty-odd miles from Sde Boker to the Mahane Yatir, and the way Gallin was driving, covering about seventeen miles every ten minutes, meant that, unless we were atomized in a crash on the way, we would get there in a little over forty-five minutes, allowing for the pit stop so she could get her feet wet and turn heavy-biblical on me.

The forest, as we entered from the parched, yellow rock and sands of the Negev desert, was nothing short of an extraordinary achievement. Though it was not perhaps what someone from the northeastern United States would think of as a forest. For us, a forest is a dark place with a dense canopy that cuts out almost all the light, and the trees grow sometimes as little as one or two feet apart. The Yatir Forest was not like that. It was a beautiful, broad, airy place with millions of pines growing maybe ten, twenty, or thirty feet apart, among beds of brown pine needles, rocks, and stones. You got the feeling as you drove through it that it was a young place, where young trees were reaching, fresh and green, for a brilliant blue sky, changing by subtle degrees the microclimate around them, calling to the rain that would eventually turn that desert green. It was a forest created by dreamers, for dreamers.

Pretty soon we began to see signs, first for the Yatir Hill, and shortly after that, the Yatir Zen Monastery and Retreat. There, we pulled off onto what was little more than a dirt track and followed it, lurching and bumping around the massive, pyramid-like hill, and pretty soon it began to climb steeply toward the summit.

Eventually we came to an esplanade where a sign invited us to leave our vehicle and finish the climb on foot. Which we did by means of a series of steps cut into the hill that wound their way to the top.

When you think of a Zen monastery, you normally picture a fortress-like building with pagoda roofs and dragons carved into them. This monastery was nothing like that. It seemed to be more like a small village made up of cabins located randomly around a large pond, maybe twenty feet across, where tall trees provided shade, and reeds and rushes grew at the edges. At the center, rather bizarrely, there was a fountain playing, and four meditating Buddhas gazed out on the four corners of the Earth.

Paths led from this central point in rambling, meandering lines, to the cabins which were located, in no apparent order, around the top of the hill. But to our left, as we came to the top of the steps and took all of this in, there was one cabin that was larger than the rest. There the door stood open, with a chair propped against it, and seemed to exude an air of administration.

"How do the Elohim feel about Zen Buddhists, Gallin?" I asked as I set off across the area toward the large cabin.

"Moses replaced the Elohim with Yahweh on Mount Horeb, as you well know."

"That whole Ehyeh, Yahweh thing."

She grunted and pushed into the office ahead of me. There were bookcases lining the walls and a black desk. Behind the desk was a bald man who might have been Japanese. He was wearing what looked like a brown robe. He watched us with seventy percent of a smile on his face. Gallin approached the desk, and I joined her.

"Good afternoon. We are looking for a friend who might have joined your monastery or come to stay here."

Blinks are not known for making a noise. But this guy actually blinked quietly. He waited for her to continue.

"His name is Drake, William Drake. Is he staying here?"

"I cannot give you that information." He had only a trace of an oriental accent.

There was a chair against the wall, and she pulled it over and sat, leaning on the desk with her elbows.

"OK," she said, "I am going to make this easy for you." That brought his smile up to eighty percent. She pulled out her card and showed it to him. "I am Captain Aila Gallin with the Mossad." She jabbed her thumb at me. "This is Alex Mason. He is with Pentagon Intelligence. We need to see William Drake very urgently. His life is at risk. Do you understand?"

"I understand, Captain Gallin. You are an important

person, you are a captain with the Mossad, and Mr. Mason has come from America representing the Pentagon. I understand that you need to see General William Drake urgently because his life may be in danger, and you want to help him. I understand all of this. But I still cannot give you the information you ask for."

"Why?"

His eyebrows rose up his forehead, and I knew he was about to enjoy wrapping Gallin in a complex, sticky web of sophistry and Zen blind alleys. So I stepped over and pulled up another chair and said, "The sound of one hand clapping is the almost inaudible sound of displaced air. Let's cut to the chase. *Entia non sunt multiplicanda praeter necesitatem.* What is stopping you from telling us where General Drake is?"

"He said to me, 'Izamu,'—Izamu is my name—'Izamu, give me your word that you will not tell anybody where I am.' And I gave him my word. So I cannot give you the information you ask for."

Gallin flopped back in her chair. "So if this man gets killed—"

That took his smile to ninety percent. I put my hand on her arm and said to Izamu, "If we give you our solemn word that we will wait for you in this office, and that we won't follow you, will you take a message to General Drake for us?"

"No."

Gallin sighed noisily, stood, and went to stand at the open door, leaning on the jamb, looking out. I watched him a moment and saw real amusement in his eyes.

"What would stop you from taking him a message?"

"I don't need to go and give you the opportunity of calculating how long I am gone so you can make a perimeter in your mind inside which General Drake must be. General Drake might be here, in the monastery, he might be in Tel Aviv or in Jerusalem. Maybe he has flown back to USA. You don't know. So you don't know if I can go and take him a message."

He was smiling. Behind me, I heard Gallin turn around to face him. Izamu went on.

"But I can send him Whatsapp message from you, and then he can decide what to do for himself."

"That would be very kind of you. Please give him our names and tell him that we come from Gabriel."

He pulled out a cell and typed very quickly with his thumbs. As he typed, he asked me, "What is the sound of something almost inaudible, Mr. Mason?" He set down his phone and looked directly into my eyes. "Is it almost a sound, or almost not a sound?"

I frowned, actually intrigued by the question. He made it to the hundred percent smile and laughed. "I am not asking you for an answer, Mr. Mason. I am just offering you a garden path for your mind while you wait for the general. The flowers are nice on that path. Please excuse me while I continue to work."

Gallin said, "I'll wait outside."

"I will let you know if he answers. There are benches by the pond. You can sit in the shade."

I thanked him, and we crossed the small esplanade to the shaded pond where the sound of the rippling water made me wonder if something almost inaudible was almost a sound or almost not a sound.

"If it was almost a sound," I said to Gallin, "it would be almost audible. So almost *in*audible is almost *not* a sound." She gave me a baleful look, but I went on regardless. "But if it was not a sound, it would be nothing, right? And how can you be almost nothing? Nothing, by definition, doesn't exist. If not existing itself is impossible, how can you *almost* not exist?"

"Shall I do it now," she said, "or shall I wait until we are somewhere remote, where nobody can hear you scream?"

She sat on a stone bench with her elbows on her knees and looked at the water. There were fat goldfish swimming among the dappled shadows and the reeds. It was a peaceful, almost reassuring sight.

A footfall behind me made me turn. He was about twenty feet from me. He was a good six foot one or two. He was strongly built and had that unmistakable military stride. He had short, sandy hair, a pale denim shirt, jeans, and leather lace-up boots. His eyes were dark blue, his gaze was keen and unwavering, and he had a cigar clamped between his teeth.

I stood, took a step toward him, and asked, "Good afternoon. Are you William Drake?"

He came to a stop six or seven feet from me and turned his head to look at Gallin as she stood up.

"You're Gabriel's daughter," he said. It wasn't a question, but she nodded and said, "Yes."

He turned to me. "And you're Nero's man."

"Are you William Drake?"

"Is it just the two of you or did you bring others with you?"

"It's just me and Gallin, and we're not supposed to be here. Please answer the question. Are you General William Drake?"

"You know damned well I am. Now you tell me, how the hell did you find me?"

SEVENTEEN

"THE SAME DAY YOU AND YOUR FAMILY WERE KILLED in a road accident in Arizona, you used the card on your numbered account in Tel Aviv and then Sde Boker. You also penciled in and then rubbed out the location of a Zen monastery on a map of Israel, which was the only piece of furniture you actually put in place in your office. The books on Budo clinched it." I said all this and then added, "Sir, you are a soldier, not a spook."

He grunted. "What do you want?"

"To talk to you in private before things get seriously out of hand."

"It's a bit late for that." He snarled it, turned, and started walking away. We followed. Over his shoulder, he snapped, "I suppose you have drawn the whole world's attention to my wife and children. I had hoped they would be hidden and secure at the kibbutz."

Gallin spoke for the first time. "We managed to deflect the attention you had drawn to them. They are now in protective custody, which is where they will stay until we can clean up this mess."

He didn't answer but kept walking down a dirt track that wound through pine copses to a cabin set back behind a front yard which was framed by tall cypress trees. He strode to the front door, opened it, and stood back to let Gallin and me in, then came in behind us and closed and locked the door. We were in an open plan living room-cum-dining room which was sparsely and unimaginatively furnished. An open door led to a small kitchen.

"Coffee?" he said, "or beer or whiskey?" He pointed to an arrangement of old chairs, a couch, and a television by a window that overlooked his back yard and said, "Sit."

Gallin, as she so often did, spoke my own thoughts. "After that drive through the desert, I could use a cold beer."

He looked at me, and I nodded. He snapped, "Three beers," like he was issuing a command to himself and went to the kitchen where he pulled three beers from his fridge. He opened them and carried them over to his sitting area, where we sat and he handed out the cold bottles.

"I am ashamed of what I allowed to happen to my life, but don't expect me to start weeping and beating my chest about it. Guilt and self-flagellation never fixed a problem yet. My feelings are my own, and nobody gets to gloat over them. What do you want to talk about?"

Gallin said, "The Cabal. When you heard that Professor Geller had been commissioned that report, you approached him and offered to help him." He took a pull on his beer, smacked his lips, and sighed. She went on, "Is there a cabal seeking to subject the United States of America, the European Union, and the United Kingdom of Great Britain and

Northern Ireland to a dystopian, totalitarian system of government, using artificial intelligence and a militarized police force? Several names are listed, including Ben J. Hyder, CEO of the Norman Swirbul Space and Aeronautics Corporation, former president Barak Hussein Obama, Mitch Hansen, CEO of the Skyhawk Defense Technology Corporation, Abraham Bellow, director of the Rat Labs, William Portos, founder of the universally used Portal Operating System, and Richard W Bramble, former director of CIA, amongst other things."

He didn't answer. I said, "So?"

"I knew Geller," he said. "I'd known Geller a long time. His IQ was off the charts, but he was emotionally unstable. So there was a limit to how far he was ever going to go in life. If he'd been a little less wild and a bit more focused, he could have become a very rich, powerful man."

"Like you?" There was ice in Gallin's voice when she asked it and sadness in Drake's smile when he nodded and said, "Yeah, like me."

He sighed and went on. "Still, Geller was a very useful man to know. He had his finger on the pulse of technological developments across the globe, and despite his eccentricities, people liked him, and he had contacts in Beijing, Moscow, Iran…" He shook his head. "You name it, he had friends in every major lab and university on the planet. So aside from the fact that I liked the son of a bitch, I stayed in touch with him because he was useful, and we often exchanged favors. He would supply me with intelligence few other people got to see, and I would see to it that funding, commissions, and contracts went his way."

He fell silent, and Gallin and I waited. After a while, he twitched his head, like he was emerging from some inner dialogue, and said, "That's corrupt. I know that, and to be honest, I don't give a damn. It's the way the world works. It always has and always will work that way as long as we are human. You know why? I'll tell you why. Because justice and fairness require equality, and human beings are not equal and never will be. Privilege goes to the best. It always has, and it always will."

Gallin snorted. "A brief look at DC or Westminster proves that is bullshit, sir, not to mention Paris, Berlin, Madrid...shall I go on?"

"Puppets! You think those clowns wield any power? Once in a generation, *maybe!* Once in a generation a member of the Cabal enters the White House with a very specific task to perform. The last Cabal member to occupy the office of Prime Minister in the United Kingdom resigned thirty-five years ago. The last Cabal member to occupy the Oval Office had the task of shifting American public opinion away from our traditional sympathy for the Jews toward a more sympathetic view of Islam."

Gallin shook her head and seemed to wince. "*Why?*"

He took a deep breath and sighed heavily. "Because we are *in* the Apocalypse, Captain. We have entered the End Times. It is not *going* to happen. It is happening as we speak."

I felt a sudden rush of anger and exploded. "More bullshit! How often do we have to listen to this garbage? Has everybody gone crazy? People are dying. People are getting killed, and you are talking about End Times and biblical prophesy? For crying out loud!"

He turned an arched eyebrow on me. "Are you seriously telling me, Mr. Mason, that you are not aware of how much the world has changed in the last twenty-five years? Are you not aware of the paranoid control exercised by Western states over individual citizens? There was an outcry in the late '90s when smoking was banned in restaurants because it was encroaching on personal liberties. We have gone so far beyond that now. Now even your car tells you what lane to drive in, how fast to go, put your damned seat belt on! The Great Social Machine now even tells you what to think! And how to think it! We even have the concept of 'Right-Thinking-People.' I know because I was at the meetings at Bilderberg and the World Economic Forums where the decisions were made to eliminate freedom of speech and through it freedom of thought! So don't tell me it's bullshit!"

Gallin said, "COVID..."

"Ha!" He gave a single, bitter laugh. "We got the whole damned Western World to clap and sing at the same time, celebrating their lockdown in their pens, like happy sheep!"

I shook my head. "This is unreal."

He snorted. "What's unreal is the blind stupidity of men like you who still believe you live in a free democracy. Democracy is *dead!* Along with all your ancient liberties, Mr. Mason."

Gallin interjected, "I need you to explain something to me."

"There at least we can agree."

"If everything you are saying is true, how come the Mossad is assisting you? Also, why the hell am I not being told about it? And why is my father is being kept out of the loop? We were assigned to find Geller and Orlev's killers and recover their report. So why were we not briefed on you and the help you're receiving from Israel?"

"OK." He nodded several times. "It's a good question. The only way I can answer it is like this. One of the ways the world has changed—let me rephrase that. One of the ways the

Cabal has changed the world is to make the enemy invisible. One of the reasons soldiers started wearing uniforms was so that you could identify your enemies and your comrades and tell them apart. But now you just don't know who your enemy is. Enemies can wear the same uniform as you, speak the same language, be of your own nationality, but inside, in their hearts and souls, they hate you and want you dead. They have a different vision of what your nation should be or what the future should hold. Today, your enemy can be anyone, anywhere. I am sitting here, talking to you, and I don't know if you are about to pull a knife or a gun and kill me. Just as you don't know whether I have had a true crisis of conscience and defected from the Cabal, or whether I am engaged in a subtle plot designed to take us to the next stage of our project."

He stubbed out his cigar in an ashtray and spoke absently, echoing what Mrs. Geller had said to us.

"'A nation can survive its fools. It can even survive the ambitious, but it cannot survive treason from within. The enemy at the gates is less formidable, for he is known, and carries his banner openly. But the traitor moves freely...' Cicero. Nobody knows this better than Israel. Israel's enemies are everywhere, and increasingly her allies are turning against her. And she stands to lose more than anybody if the Cabal's plans reach fulfillment."

Gallin snapped, "Why?"

"Because fundamentalist Islam is key to the next stage."

I got to my feet and half-shouted, "*You're out of your mind!* Do you really think we are going to buy this bullshit? You really think we are going to believe this is what was on that flash drive?"

He stared at me for a long moment. "Was?" He turned to look at Gallin. "You haven't got the drive?"

She remained expressionless. I said, "Right now, like Cicero, I don't know who my friends or my enemies are. So I am not inclined to tell you where the flash drive is."

"I made it absolutely clear to Nero that it was imperative the drive was recovered."

"Was that before or after you made a secret deal with the Mossad? I'll tell you what I think, General. I think you're talking a lot of bull. You seriously want us to believe that fundamentalist Islam is going to—"

He interrupted me. "Ask any mullah, any imam, they will all tell you plainly that there is no such thing as fundamentalist Islam. There is just Islam, the word of God as received by Mohamed. You cannot interpret it. It is as it is expressed in the Koran."

Gallin rose to the bait. "What about the terrorists who murder and rape women and children and torture and murder men simply because they are not Muslims?"

"Tell me, Captain Gallin," he asked quietly, "one single place in the Western world today where you could ask that question without being publicly reviled by all the mainstream media, or even run the risk of prosecution." He leaned forward and stared at each of us in turn. "Understand this, get this into your heads: We have engineered this. Sharia law will be incorporated into Western law. Not by statute but by default. Because nobody will dare oppose it. Why do we want Islam to spread across the West? The name itself says it. Islam means subjugation.

"There are too many people on this planet, Mr. Mason. We need another flood, but until that comes along, we need these nine billion people to be mentally, emotionally, and physically *crippled!* Living in fear of expressing anything like a personal opinion or a protest." He laughed. "Unless of course it's a protest against Western imperialism and oppression. We are *deliberately* moving toward a dystopian society where freedom of expression, free speech, free exercise of any of the ancient liberties will be *de facto* forbidden and ultimately outlawed, and where necessary severely punished. There will be absolute electronic and AI control. The human adventure is over, Mr. Mason. *Ewige Blumenkraft und ewige Schlangenkraft!*"

I ignored the reference and asked, "Can you prove any of this?"

"Yes, several times over and in great detail."

I narrowed my eyes at him, trying to read him. "But if you are a part of this, what made you defect?"

He fell silent, turning the bottle of beer around in his hands. After a moment, he pulled a cigar from his breast pocket and lit it with a box of matches. When it was going, he started to talk with puffs of smoking wafting from his mouth.

"The Cabal has been around a long time. Only the top five know exactly how long, but at the very least since 1947. When they recruited me, the story they sold me was that the purpose of the Cabal was to ensure that America would take its place in the world as the number one superpower, to ensure the world as a whole moved toward peace, prosperity, democracy, and the rule of law. They were things I believed in, and I signed up. I wasn't crazy about the whole ritualistic side." He glanced at us both, like he wondered how we would react to the idea of rituals. "They have a few rituals. Like the Masons, they say they date back all the way to Solomon. Not my style, but it goes with the territory, I guess."

He shrugged. "Anyhow, the more I advanced up through the ranks, which I did pretty quickly, the more I began to see that the whole story they had sold me was just that, a story. Postwar America was a convenient place for them to establish themselves because any fool could see that with the nation's resources and the free market economy, the United States was going to be the richest, most powerful nation on the planet. If the Cabal had existed forty or fifty years before that, they would without a doubt have been based in Britain.

"But by the time this started to dawn on me, I owed them my houses, my apartments, my cars, my yacht, my career, my children's education..." He sighed. "It was easier to justify what I knew in terms of their promoting and defending a fundamentally Anglo-Saxon system of parliamentary democracy based on the Magna Carta and Henry VIII's Reformation, two institutions which are as much ours as Britain's. And slowly, bit by bit, my American patriotism became a generalized, vague patriotism of the West.

"Then October 7th happened. And I saw how the Cabal manipulated the media and the press, with very few and notable exceptions, into presenting those murderous aggressors as victims. These men hammered nails into women's legs while they were raping them. They amputated parts of women's bodies and played catch with them. The atrocities they committed were worthy of the worst Nazi atrocities during the war, and no one, from Washington to London to the United Nations in New York, no one stood up to condemn those bastards and stand by Israel in her fight for survival. Oh sure!"

He raised both hands like I'd pulled a gun on him. "We have our aircraft carriers out there, the *Theodore Roosevelt* and the *Abe Lincoln*, and there are a couple of subs out there too.

But let's be clear: Israel is *alone* out there on the front line in a war where Israel *and* the United States *and* the United Kingdom are the primary targets. Israel stands alone, defending *us*. And we are honor bound. We should have boots on the ground in Lebanon and Gaza, and Syria and Iran, and we should be unequivocal in our support. But we are not." He stared at us both in turn. "Why?"

I gave a small shrug. "I had always assumed it was politicians playing footsy with oil producers."

He shook his head. "We are the major oil producer on the planet, and we are more than capable of taking control of Middle Eastern oil if we wanted to. No. The Middle East has something a lot more attractive than oil. It has Islam!"

EIGHTEEN

I sat shaking my head. Gallin was watching me, chewing her lip, and General Drake was looking like he was trying not to look mad.

"You're not selling it," I told him. "You're trying to sell a conspiracy theory, and I'm not buying. OK, men in power go a bit crazy. Or maybe they need to be crazy to get there in the first place. And sure, in the past there have been some really crazy people in power."

I paused, nodding, and raised my hand to stop them interrupting. "Yes, we all know about the Masons and how much power they wield, and we all know the Illuminati really existed. But we also know that the Masons work within the system, and for every judge who lets off a fellow Mason, another doubles the sentence to teach him a lesson; and we also know that the Illuminati were crushed by the Bavarian government. Secret societies do not prosper, General. You know why? Because if they were as powerful as you would like us to believe, they wouldn't need to be secret.

"The Third Reich was powerful, it was not secret. The Soviet Union was very powerful, it was not secret. Franco's regime in Spain was a conspiracy that succeeded. It ruled the country, not in secret but openly, because it was powerful. True power does not need to hide in the shadows. Secrecy is a product of fear, General. So what is your Cabal afraid of, that won't let it come into the open?"

He nodded, with his eyes on the bottle in front of him.

"What I am trying to tell you, Mr. Mason, is that the Cabal is emerging from secrecy because it has acquired that power."

"So what the hell does it need Islam for?"

"Do you know what Hitler said about Islam?"

I sighed. "No, amaze me."

"He said, both in public and in private, that it was both a religion and a political ideology that was admirable, because it was more disciplined, militaristic, and political than Christianity. He and Himmler commended Mohammed as a politician and a military leader. Islam is all about blind, unthinking obedience.

"We have all seen how Christianity has fragmented into hundreds of sects, each trying to reach Christ's true message and trying to square his teachings of peace and love with the brutality of the Old Testament, and we all know that Judaism is anything but unthinking. But Islam? Absolute subjugation to an unforgiving god. It is founded on unquestioning obedience to Mohammed and those who speak for him. There are no sects, there is no interpretation. This is what he said, this is what you do."

"Yeah, we know that. What's your point?"

"The population of this planet in 1947 was less than two and a half billion. Today we are crowding the critical tipping point of nine billion. I don't know if either of you has ever thought about this." He arched an eyebrow that said he was pretty sure we hadn't. "But the more people you have, the more difficult democracy becomes. Democracy—rule by the majority to limit the tyranny of the minority—becomes the rule of the marginalized minorities over an increasingly powerless majority. Look around you. One by one, your ancient liberties are being eroded away to protect some faction of society that the authorities tell you is underrepresented. The voice of the individual is lost, replaced by the voice of the group, the faction, the ideology, the religion. It doesn't matter if it's Black women or, increasingly, white men, lesbians, gays, transsexuals, transsexual homosexuals…" He shook his head. "You name it. Individuals have lost their voices and can only be heard through a collective group that represents them. And enter into this overcrowded mass of conflicting collectives all drooling over their cell phones in search of an opinion to espouse as though it were their own, Islam."

He stared at Gallin like he was wondering whether she was hearing him. Then he turned to me.

"Have you noticed, by the way, how in recent years every Western government has been so eager to import millions of Muslims? Nine percent of New Yorkers are Muslims. Fifteen percent of London is Muslim, but take a city like Bradford in the United Kingdom, and thirty percent of the population is Muslim. About fifteen percent of Paris, eleven percent in Berlin, a quarter of Stockholm's population is Muslim. And please note that we are talking about refugees who build mosques and live in Muslim communities. They represent a very powerful, committed force."

"So what," I said with heavy sarcasm, feeling a building

anger in my gut, "you're saying that if Muslims represent five or ten percent of Western society they are going to take over the remaining ninety to ninety-five percent and impose Sharia law?"

"That is not an intelligent question, Mason."

I stopped dead because the reply had not come from the general. It had come from Gallin. She went on.

"General Drake is not saying that. What he is saying is that in an environment of crisis or unrest—a false flag, a purported external threat, war with Russia and North Korea in Europe— if emergency laws had to be invoked, a ten percent Muslim population could become a very powerful ally if they were promised that Sharia law might be respected and or incorporated into national law. It sounds insane to us today, but it would be insanely easy to trigger a situation like that. Look how quickly and easily everybody adapted to the changes after nine-eleven and COVID. The New Normal."

"I think you're both out of your minds." I stared at him. "I think you're playing us. I can't believe Nero buys into this crap. You say you have proof?"

"Conclusive proof."

I stood and walked to the window. Then turned and jabbed a finger at him.

"I have to tell you, General, I am no fan of Islam, but what I am hearing from you sounds just as bad. It sounds to me like hysterical, xenophobic garbage designed to whip up paranoia and hatred."

He shrugged. "Maybe you're right. In fact, you probably are. I am not trying to sell you my world view. What I am telling you is that there is a cabal, of which I was a high-ranking member, who have chosen to confront the three major problems of our time"—he held up his hand and counted them out on his fingers—"massive overpopulation, climate change, and artificial intelligence, by creating a totalitarian society where the elite live in a kind of Eden paradise on Earth while a mindless, subservient humanity serves them and keeps them there. And one of the tools they plan to use to keep them there is some variation based on Islam. Just look around you, Mason. Look at how the world has changed in less than a single lifetime. Do you think a person living in the '60s, the '70s, the '80s—hell! even the '90s, would recognize the world today? It's not going to become a dystopia. It already *is* a dystopia, and it can only get worse. You tell me! Tell me one single force on this planet today driving us to a better outcome."

I sighed loudly and shook my head. I didn't answer because I couldn't. Instead I said, "What's this conclusive proof you say you have?"

He turned and looked at Gallin, who was sitting very quietly looking at the floor.

He said, "You know I'm right, don't you? You've been at the front line. You know how mindless people can become when you program them right."

He got to his feet and came to where I stood by the window.

"I need to know what happened to the flash drive. You were tasked with recovering it. You autonomously changed your mission without consulting with Nero, and you came to seek me out. Why?"

I was about to tell him to go to hell, but Gallin broke in.

"An agent had recovered it. He was captured and tortured and then assassinated. Mason shot the assassin through the heart. It was a pretty amazing shot, but the assassin had the flash drive in his left breast pocket."

General Drake closed his eyes and sighed deeply. "So it was destroyed."

I gave Gallin a look that said we'd talk later and said, "Yes."

"I have documents, hard copies. I was the chief treasurer for the Cabal, and I had access to their bank accounts in Switzerland, Panama, and a string of other offshore locations. I have the account numbers and the access codes. I also have key printouts, memos, and documents going back years, listing names, events, payoffs. It is all stuff that would be impossible to falsify. If this stuff got into the open, backed by people powerful enough, like Nero, like me, it could bring down the Cabal. It would also bring devastation to Western society."

He waited. I didn't say anything, so he went on.

"I also have emails, photographs, videos"—he paused, shaking his head—"thousands of documents on my hard drive. It is what I offered Geller and Orlev. If we can get this into the right hands, maybe we can do something to stop this slide toward a totalitarian dystopia. Maybe. But Captain Gallin was right. We've had nine-eleven, and we've had COVID. The third one will be a false flag, and then it will be too late. It is already in the making in Ukraine, with North Korea and Iran. You have to believe me, Mason, and we need to act."

He turned and walked away toward a staircase that rose to the upper floor. There he stopped and looked back at me.

"I am going to get the material. While I am gone, ask yourself why Orlev and Geller were murdered. Why was your agent tortured and killed? Why did Nero send you on this crazy goose chase in the first place?"

He climbed the stairs. I could feel Gallin looking at me. I didn't return the look because I was feeling too mad.

She said, "He's right. You know that."

I didn't look at her. "You shouldn't have told him the drive was destroyed."

"You can't see that has ceased to be relevant?"

I still couldn't look at her. She got to her feet and came and stood in front of me. She grabbed my face and forced me to look into her eyes.

"Mason, listen to me. Just a hundred miles north of here, war is raging on our northern border. But we are fighting proxies—Iranian and Russian proxies. Our enemies—the United States, The United Kingdom and Israel's enemies—are Russia and Iran. So why are our closest allies holding back? Think about it! How hard would it be, in this situation, facing Putin and the Ayatollah, who can't wait to drop a nuclear bomb on us, how hard would it be to pull a false flag and institute martial law? Do I need to paint a picture?"

"This is bullshit!"

"Especially with North Korean troops now in Ukraine!"

"It's bullshit!"

"It's not bullshit, Mason!"

"There has to be another, more rational explanation for what is happening. I do not believe—I *will not* believe that there is a conspiracy at the heart of Western governments to institute a totalitarian dictatorship using Muslims as some kind of Trojan Horse thought police. It is too crazy!"

Her face showed anger but also disappointment, which made me feel like crap.

"Yeah? Well let me tell you, pal. I was abducted and taken

to Iran, and I had to cross that country and escape to Turkey[1], and I can tell you that that totalitarian dystopia you believe is too crazy to exist already exists. And it would be all too easy for it to spread like a plague through Western Europe and the United States. Precisely"—and she stabbed her finger into my chest—"because of the complacency of men like you."

"Hey!" I scowled. "Take it easy!"

"Let me tell you something, buster!" She stabbed me on the chest again with her finger. "In the UK, *right now, as we speak*, in the cradle of parliamentary democracy, workers' rights and equality laws are being updated to make employers liable for staff being offended by third parties. Said like that, it's kind of meaningless, right? But what it *means*, what it actually *means* in day-to-day reality, is that when you go to the pub, or a restaurant, or you go shopping or pop into the baker's for a loaf of bread, the owner of that establishment is responsible for controlling your conversation and making sure you do not express any thoughts that might be offensive to his staff! So if his staff are Muslims, you are in trouble. Why? Because he has become the thought police. And before you brush that aside, let me remind you that just a couple of months ago, a guy was jailed for two years in the UK for dressing up as a Jihadist bomber at a Halloween party. You know what the crime was? Shall I tell you? It was using a public communication network to send an offensive message. Is that dystopian enough for you?"

She turned, took two steps, and came back to thump me on the chest with the heel of her hand. "Tell me this: If I publish a book which is critical of Islamic ideology, that says it

---

1. See *Alex Mason 3, Mason's Law*

is not OK to sentence people to death for converting to another religion, is that using a public communication network to send an offensive message? Should I go to prison for that? Are we getting dystopian enough for you, Mason?"

"Dial it down, Gallin."

"We are losing our freedom, Mason! Our liberties, rights, and freedoms are being systematically dismantled by a clique of ruthless bastards who are setting themselves up as a pantheon of billionaire demigods who do what the hell they like while we are told what we can and cannot think!"

"OK."

I heard a creak on the stair. Gallin gave me a look that was somewhere between pleading and murderous and turned away. General Drake was standing halfway down the stairs. He was holding a suitcase and a laptop and watching us. He smiled and came the rest of the way down.

"I wish I had your gift for self-expression, Captain. I could not have said it better myself if I had spent all night with a speech writer." He dropped the case beside his chair and put the laptop on the coffee table. "That is exactly what I wanted to communicate to you, Mason. And let me tell you, when you have finished looking at this material, you will know it's true. It is already a reality."

I watched him a moment. "And you were one of them."

"I was." He didn't look at me.

"You've given up a lot of privilege for the sake of your principles."

"Not as much as you might think." He still wouldn't look at me. "I have taken little in the way of material benefits. I have devoted myself mainly to work."

"Just a couple of houses, apartments, a plane, a yacht..."

"My wife and my kids. It was all for them. What I did, what I got out of it, was the belief that I was protecting my country and the ideals on which it was founded. Maybe that sounds corny to you, Mr. Mason, but they happen to be things I believe in." He pointed to the stuff on the table. "You want to sit down and go through this?"

I watched him for a moment, while Gallin watched me. I nodded.

"Yeah, let's see the proof."

NINETEEN

THE PROOF WAS, AS HE HAD SAID IT WOULD BE, irrefutable. We sat there for a full six hours going through the whole lot of it in minute detail. There was everything from the assassination of presidents to engineered crashes of the economy, the facilitating of terrorist attacks, and the invasion of sovereign nations to protect the national interest. What was most harrowing of all was the complete list of the thirty-two men and women who constituted the three tiers of what they called the *Ma'agel Pnimi Kdush*, or the Sacred Inner Circle. This is turn was divided into *Chamsha Kadusha*, or the Sacred Five, *Tsha Hakdushim*, or the Sacred Nine, and *Ben Hitmona Shmona Esra*, or the Mortal Eighteen. The Sacred Five were in turn divided into *Arba'at ha' amudim*, or the Four Pillars, and *Ha'in*, or the Eye.

There were many members and associate members besides these. But these, particularly the Five and the Nine, constituted the true Cabal. The guys who were in the know.

By the time we had finished, it was practically midnight,

and I felt mentally, physically, and emotionally exhausted. I sagged back in my chair and rubbed my face with my hands. I might have just thought it, or I might have said it. I felt like my entire life up to that point had been amputated. Everything I had ever believed in or taken as solid reality had suddenly flickered, like the black cat in the Matrix, and the whole edifice, the whole tower of my world had suddenly crumbled. Everything I had ever believed in was a lie.

The general surprised me by smiling.

"You look like you need a whiskey." He paused, and the smile faded. "They got me when I was young. They saw potential in me. So I had years to adapt, but even so, it still shakes me when I allow myself to think of the implications. I can't imagine what it's like for you, getting it all in one go. It's hard to assimilate."

I watched his face, his expression, still wondering if it was genuine or an act.

"Nero knows about this? All of this that you have just shown us?"

"Of course. He's spent his entire career trying to get proof. More to the point, he's spent the last thirty-odd years trying to find out what he could do with that proof if he ever got it."

He stood and took a cigar from his breast pocket. He stuck in between his teeth and pulled a box of matches from his jeans. He gave a dry laugh as he struck one and puffed.

"But Mason," he said when he had it burning, "when you think about it, who *doesn't* know about it? Go to any bar on any street in the Western World, and they'll be talking about it. Some will talk in terms of conspiracy, the Military Industrial Intelligence Complex, the Illuminati, the Masons, the Communists or the Neo Fascists, World Government, New

World Order, hell! UAPs! Others will talk about an Orwellian machine that acquires some kind of life of its own. Not a conscious conspiracy but an inevitable consequence of a bloated society, an economy built on a vacuum of credit. But it all boils down to the same thing in the end: an elite who manipulate the economy and world events to their own ends to secure not wealth but power. We all know it's there, everyone knows it's happening, *everyone* feels increasingly powerless in the face of this megalithic monster, but only the crazies have the courage to come out and talk about it."

He waved a dismissive hand at me. "Bah! What's the point? You want that whiskey?"

"Yeah. I need it."

"Captain?"

"I'm in."

He left the room and went into the kitchen. Gallin sighed and eyed me sidelong.

"Hey, big guy. I owe you an apology."

"I let you down."

"You didn't. This is a pretty crazy place we're at. Somebody has to keep their feet on the ground. Even if they're wrong. You keep me grounded. I need that sometimes."

"Thanks, Gallin. I appreciate it. Now you can help me decide what the hell we do with all this."

She smiled on the right side of her face. "That's easy. We throw it at the fan and duck."

"OK." I nodded. "But following your metaphor, what, exactly, precisely, is the fan? Because if we go in all crazy, we could very easily end up throwing it all down the can."

The smile continued. "I think you are taking my metaphor too far, but I hear what you're saying."

The general emerged from the kitchen with a bottle of Macallan and three tumblers. As he set them down and poured, he said, "I went to a lot of trouble to escape from the United States. Now you're going to take me back?"

Gallin shook her head. "I don't see why. We're all agreed Israel does not pose a threat. Stay here with armed protection. Let Nero come here. We debrief you."

The general shook his head, then pointed at me with his glass.

"He knows why not."

Gallin arched an eyebrow at me. "You do?"

I nodded. "I see a couple of reasons. The first is that there is obvious compartmentalized division within the Mossad itself and possibly the administration. I am not sure how much good will and trust there is between Israel and the United States right now, or how willing they would be to share any intelligence they derive from the general. I can't say I blame them. They have been betrayed by their closest allies, besides which, like the general said earlier, this is a time when your enemy might be your own commanding officer. They might share this stuff with an American CIA officer who just happens to be working for Tehran or Moscow, or the Military Industrial Intelligence Complex, or the Cabal. They just don't know. By the time Nero gets here, the general could have vanished."

She made a doubtful face but then nodded. "OK."

"A second point is that we three might just make it to DC unnoticed. The chances of Nero making it to Tel Aviv, let alone the Yatir Forest, without being spotted and shot are remote, to say the least. He is probably under twenty-four hour surveillance. Our enemy has the very best next generation black technology at their disposal."

She nodded again. "True. So what do you suggest?"

"We go old school. We go dark."

She smiled. "I like the sound of it. What does it mean in terms of nuts and bolts?"

"Broad brushstrokes, we leave discreetly in a vehicle which is not ours, we head for the coast, we steal a yacht, head for Cyprus, and fly from there to DC."

The general said, "I might be able to help there, but I am very much in two minds about it. It could be a blessing, or it could be a curse in disguise."

I turned in my seat to look at him. "What is it?"

"I have a friend, Dave, David Rappaport. He is a billionaire, though he counts his billions in single digits, and he is only in the outer circle of the Cabal. He has a couple of yachts and keeps a small one, a Horizon E18 if memory serves, at Ashkelon. He has often lent it to me, and the staff at the Marina know me and will think nothing of my going onboard."

Gallin said, "Ashkelon. It's fifty miles west of here and has a luxury yacht marina. You can't take boats out right now because of the war in Gaza and Lebanon, but I can make a call."

"We don't want anyone to know what we're doing. Not the Mossad, not the CIA, not even ODIN."

She shook her head. "They don't need to know what we're doing. They just need to know it's me and not to shoot me."

I turned suddenly on the general, feeling a sudden stab of anger and irritation.

"Why the hell didn't you do this from the start, General? Why the hell did you come to Israel and then, instead of going to Glilot and seeking the protection of the Mossad, come and hide in a damned Zen monastery? Why didn't you go straight to ODIN in the first place?" I pointed at him, feeling the hot coals of frustration in my gut. "You are playing some kind of game. It stinks to high heaven, and you are making me *very* nervous!"

He and Gallin both stared at me for a long moment. Finally he sighed.

"The only game I am playing is trying to keep my wife and children alive and safe. If I had gone straight to Nero in DC, my wife and children would have been dead within twenty-four hours—if they were lucky! The only way open to me was to give my evidence to Geller and disappear, preferably presumed dead. That's what I did, but as you pointed out to me, I am a soldier, not a spook, and you were able to find me." His weary expression turned to a scowl, and he added, "One thing I can guarantee, Mason, is that if the Cabal had orchestrated this, they would have done a far better job than I have."

Gallin nodded. "I buy that. Mason, the bottom line is that we have no time, and we have to commit one way or another. We either take him or we kill him and take the evidence."

I scowled at her. She knew as well as I did that was something we were not going to do.

"Fine. Do you trust the security coordinator?"

She shrugged. "As much as I trust anyone. If he was working for the Cabal, we'd be dead by now."

"So do we take his Land Rover and leave him our Grenadier, or do we steal a car?"

"We'll get farther if we take his. If we steal one, we risk the police being alerted. I'll go talk to him. I stay at his place and he brings the truck here. The general slips in the back and lies on the floor. He brings it and the general back to his place. I get in.

You take our vehicle and go to the hotel. Check into our room. Park somewhere visible but not too obvious. I'll take the security coordinator's Land Rover to the hotel, and you get in. Try not to look like you. We'll cruise around town to see if we're being followed, and if we're not, we'll take off and make a roundabout route to Ashkelon. There we steal Dave Rappaport's yacht."

I nodded. "Good. It makes sense."

Men make plans so the gods can laugh. Never was a truer word spoken.

Somewhere in my peripheral hearing, there was a crunch. Then there was another, like tires on dirt. I stared at Gallin. She was staring back at me. I said to the general, "You came here by car from Sde Boker."

"Of course."

"Did you disable your GPS?" He gaped, hesitated, frowned. I snapped, "*God damn it!*" and dragged him to the floor, hissing at him, "Stay down! Don't make a sound." Gallin was down on one knee, aiming her piece at the front door. There were footsteps outside, maybe three, maybe four people. The handle turned and rattled. I whispered to the general, "*Kitchen door, locked or unlocked?*"

His eyes went wide. "*Unlocked.*"

"*Stay!*"

What we needed was these bastards, whoever they were, to give up and go away and let us get the hell out of there according to our plan, but any hope of that disappeared as I heard at least two sets of boots moving toward the back of the house. These guys were not here to deliver brownies or borrow sugar. They meant to come inside the house.

I got to my feet and moved quickly and silently to the

kitchen. In the top drawer, I found a large kitchen knife with a broad blade. I flattened myself against the wall beside the back door and listened without breathing as I heard the boots approach.

I heard the front door handle rattle again, saw Gallin stiffen, and a voice called out, "*Open the door!*"

A voice from outside the kitchen shouted, "*Give me a minute, will ya! I'm comin'!*"

Both voices had American accents. Neither of them sounded particularly Israeli. Gallin glanced at me over her shoulder and shrugged. It was a 'What do we do?' shrug. We were assuming they were here to kill the general, but we didn't know. And killing four Mossad agents was not going to help anybody. I pointed to one side, telling her to get out of sight. She grabbed the general, and they moved to the side.

The kitchen door swung open. For a moment, nothing happened. Then I saw the muzzle of a semi-automatic inch past the edge of the door. A voice said, "I don't like it. The cars are outside. Where are the bastards?"

The voice that answered said, "I'm gonna let Zack and Jimmy in. You check upstairs. We want the general alive. Kill the other two."

"On my own?"

"Yeah, on your own, chicken shit! We'll be right behind you, dumbass."

I had my answer. Bigmouth moved into the kitchen with his weapon held out in front of him. A moment later Chicken-shit appeared behind him. I knew what was going to happen next. Bigmouth was going to go to the door, and Chickenshit was going to check the kitchen before going upstairs, and that was—almost—what happened. Because Bigmouth moved across the floor toward the front door, but Chickenshit only got to make a quarter of a turn before I clapped my hand over his mouth, pressing my index finger up to cover his nostrils, and rammed the point of the kitchen knife deep into the side of his neck, severing his carotid artery and his jugular vein. When the knife was in up to the hilt, I punched forward, severing his windpipe, but by that time, he was already dead.

As I lowered him to the floor, I heard the double crack of a semi-automatic and looked up to see Bigmouth slump to the floor. Two seconds passed real slow. Then there was a loud crack, and the lock on the front door exploded inward. Neither Gallin nor I opened fire. It would have been a stupid waste of ammo. They knew we were there, and they would be out of our line of fire.

For five long seconds, there was absolute silence. Then I reached back and slammed the kitchen door. There was a shout outside. The front door burst open, and I plugged Zack or Jimmy twice in the chest and ran forward, knowing, as I knew Gallin did, that the other half of the pair was legging it around the back of the cabin.

I burst out, covering the corner while she dragged the general out and hurled him in the back of the Grenadier. When she had the engine running, I kicked the front door open, knelt, and fired as the remaining Zack or Jimmy burst through the kitchen. He fell back, but I didn't see a lot of blood. I stood and hesitated. Gallin was shouting at me, "*Leave it! Let's go!*"

I should have gone in and finished him. It would have delayed us thirty seconds or a minute maximum. I knew he was hit. I just had to cross the living room, finish him, and run. Then jump in the Grenadier and get the hell out of there. But that's the thing with split-second judgment calls. Fifty percent of the time they are wrong. So I turned, swung into the passenger seat, and we pulled away. She killed the lights, and we sped off, down the road away from the house. I looked back and saw him silhouetted at the front door, clutching his shoulder.

And talking on his cell.

I snarled, "I should have gone back and finished him."

She didn't answer for a moment. Her face said she knew we'd made a mistake. "We need to get out of here fast. We don't know how many more of them there are."

"He was at the door watching us leave. He was talking on his cell."

We fishtailed out onto Highway 40, and she accelerated fast.

I said, "We go to Be'er Sheva. That's maybe fifteen minutes. If we see anyone following us on the way, we stop and kill them. We don't stop at Be'er Sheva. We drive on to Rahat. That's another ten or fifteen minutes. There we dump the Grenadier, take its plates, steal an anonymous car, and swap the plates."

She nodded. "OK, good. Another twenty minutes."

"Then instead of going west to the coast, we go east to Kseifa."

"Another quarter of an hour."

"Then south to..." I tried to visualize the map. She said, "Ar'ara BaNegev, another five minutes."

"Then we take it nice and steady, not drawing attention to ourselves, fifty-odd miles on Highway 25 to Ashkelon. A little over half an hour. Say three quarters of an hour."

"That's one hour fifty-five minutes. Call it two hours. We dump the car in a multistory car park and walk to the marina."

She sighed and for a moment looked exhausted. "From there we make it up as we go along."

And she accelerated into the night, headed north for Be'er Sheva, while far above us, the gods were rolling in the aisles, wiping the tears of mirth from their eyes.

TWENTY

As we approached the turnoff for Tlalim, we began to hear the thud of rotors overhead. I lowered the window and peered out over the blackness of the desert. Pretty soon, I saw the winking lights of a chopper. Watching it for a minute or two, I realized it was describing a grid pattern.

"It's searching for us," I said. "It thinks we've taken to the desert. It's searching the desert tracks." I turned to Gallin. "You need to put your headlights on. If it spots us with them off, we'll be sitting ducks."

"If I switch them on out here, they'll spot us straight away. I'll pull in to Tlalim, switch them on as we cruise through the streets."

I nodded. "If they decide to check the highway, they'll recognize the Grenadier."

"There's nothing we can do about that right now. Tlalim is too small to steal a car. It's a kibbutz. People in kibbutz look out for each other."

She slowed as we approached the turnoff onto the 2104

and began to approach the small desert settlement. Through the window, I could see the bright headlight of the chopper approaching. I raised the window and said, "He's right behind us. Wait till he turns before you switch on the lights."

Even as I said it, the cab was suddenly flooded by the powerful glow from a spotlight. The noise of the rotors shook the whole vehicle, and the few trees by the side of the road bowed and tossed in the downdraft. Then the light vanished, and the sound of the rotors receded.

I stared at Gallin. She was staring at me. I said, "They recognized us. Does this car have GPS?"

"Of course not."

"We need to get the hell out of here."

The car suddenly surged, and we hurtled down the road we were on, leapt over a sidewalk, and smacked down in the sand, undergrowth, and deep shadows of the desert. I heard a cry of pain from the back of the truck and made a mental note never to say, "We need to get the hell out of here" to Gallin again. Ever.

As we thundered, jumped, and jerked across the sand, potholes, and shrubs I yelled, "*Do we have anything other than hand guns in this truck?*"

"*No! Hold on!*"

I gripped wherever I could, heard the general curse, and next thing, we hit a bank and for a few timeless seconds we were in mid air. Then we hit the blacktop, the tires screamed, and the cabin filled with the light from headlights behind us. A horn blared, and the engine of the amazing Grenadier roared as we surged forward doing a hundred and twenty along Highway 40 toward Be'er Sheva.

Gallin snapped, "Where's the chopper?"

I opened the window and craned my neck out. "I don't see it."

The general's voice said, "It's behind us, a couple of miles away and closing."

I said, "Stay down."

"It's moving to our right."

I said, "It's going to come alongside us."

It was closing fast, and as I stared out the open window, I could see a guy leaning out the open door with what looked like an assault rifle. Gallin swore, "We are sitting ducks!"

I pulled my Sig and snapped at the general, "Is there anyone behind us? Any cars?"

"At this speed? Are you kidding? No!"

I turned to Gallin, but before I could say anything, a shower of burning lead smacked and rattled into the right side of the vehicle. The car swerved, but she didn't flinch. "It's bulletproof, but it won't take a lot more of that!"

In a split second, I looked at the speedometer and in my mind saw the guy changing his magazine. She was doing a hundred and thirty. I yelled, "*When I say, slam on the brakes!*"

I leaned out the window holding the Sig in both hands. I saw the guy smack the base of the magazine and put the rifle to his shoulder. I bellowed, "*Now!*" and emptied the Sig two hundred feet in front of the chopper as the tires of the Grenadier screamed and burned into the blacktop. Ahead of us, plumes of asphalt erupted from the road. Seventy yards to our right, and now two or three hundred feet ahead of us, the rifleman was tumbling into the void as the chopper weaved and began to spin down into the desert.

Gallin slammed her foot down on the gas, and we took off again with the Grenadier beast surging fast toward a hundred.

And over to our right, behind a sandy hill, a huge explosion blasted the air, and a swirling, incandescent mushroom of flames thundered into the black night sky. As we roared along Highway 40, climbing back toward a hundred and twenty, she snarled, "What the hell was that? Aside from, like, *amazing!* What the hell *was* that?"

I shrugged and grinned. "A flash of mental arithmetic told me a hundred and thirty miles per hour was between a hundred and ninety and two hundred feet per second. If I aimed two hundred feet ahead of the chopper and you stopped when I fired..."

"They would miss us by a hundred and fifty feet, allowing for stopping time, and they would fly right into your hail of lead. Man, that is *so* good." She turned and gave me a very unsettling grin. "That is *hot!*"

Fifteen minutes later, we were slowing as we moved through the suburbs of Be'er Sheva. We followed Highway 25 through the city until we came to a huge mall on the left. Even at that time of night, the city lights were blazing and the traffic was bustling. We turned in to the mall, and Gallin said, "This place is open till late. We'll look for an old model Toyota or something everybody has." As we moved slowly into the parking lot, she went on, "When we find it, you take the wheel of the Grenadier and wait. When I pull out, you pull in, then jump in the car. Got it?"

"Got it."

We spent five minutes cruising around the parking lot till she found what she wanted. It was a four-year-old Hyundai i20. There was nothing you could say about it except that it was red. She stopped the Grenadier just short of the Hyundai's trunk and opened her door. "Take the wheel."

We both jumped down, and I got in the driver's seat. I saw her hunker down, concealed by the Grenadier, and realized she was removing the plates from the Hyundai. She was fast and efficient. I had expected her to remove the plates from the Grenadier, and that worried me because she would have been in full view. Instead she swapped the plates with the car right next to it. Then she slipped some kind of key in the lock, waited thirty seconds, and the Hyundai's lights flashed and bleeped. She climbed in, pulled out of the space, and I drove in.

I heard the general climb out of the back, and as he slipped in the back seat of the car we'd just stolen, I got in the front passenger seat and we cruised slowly out of the mall and back onto Highway 25 like nothing had just happened. As we moved sedately along the highway, she held up a fob with a key hanging from it.

"I'll get you one for Christmas. You slip it in the lock. It tells the car everything is fine and just to do as it's told. The car believes it and treats it like it's its own key. They're useful. I'm surprised Nero didn't give you one."

"The only thing Nero ever gave me, apart from impossible instructions, was a headache."

"I hear you. OK, so we are forty miles, half an hour, from our objective. Judgment call, do we trust that we have lost our pursuers and go for the boat now, or do we drive all over southwestern Israel for a few hours to make sure we *have* lost them, and *then* go for the boat?"

The general spoke from the back. It was the first thing he'd said in several hours that wasn't an oath.

"You shot down the chopper, Mason. I have seen a lot of superb shooting in my time, but I have never seen that done before. They will need time to recover from that. They are operating in a hostile jurisdiction, and they are having to pull a lot of strings, which will draw attention to them, and that is one thing they really don't want here. All of this means that you have bought yourselves time. Certainly time enough to get to Ashkelon.

"And there's another thing to consider. That plate switch you did was smooth. They'll see the original plates on the Grenadier. So there is every chance they'll be looking for the plates of the car that was in that spot. Once they get around to seeing the security footage, if they ever do, we'll be halfway across the Med. I'd say you've bought yourselves many hours, if not days. My vote, if it counts for anything, is we go get the yacht."

I looked at Gallin. She gave her head a twitch. We were leaving the lights of the city behind us, and the darkness of the desert was closing in again. I said, "It makes sense, and the sooner we get this done, the better."

"OK, agreed. Let's do it."

Our first objective was to get through the desert and arrive at Ashkelon alive and uninjured. With the chopper down, that looked like becoming an actual possibility. To make matters more interesting, Ashkelon sits right on the northern edge of Gaza, and just twenty miles away from us as we hurtled along the highway, I could see several choppers moving in predatory search patterns over the area.

As I thought about the implications of that, especially after we had launched the yacht, I heard the first of the fighter-bombers that night screaming overhead, going north toward Lebanon, and soon afterward, the northern horizon began to light up like there was an electric storm approaching.

There was no doubt the conflict could work for us as a

major distraction and render any aerial search impossible. Also, once we reached Ashkelon, we would become invisible—an anonymous car in a city of a hundred and fifty thousand people. But once we got out on the sea, that would be a whole different ball game. Granted the Israeli authorities might let us pass thanks to Gallin's authority and that of her dad, but what of the Cabal? We would be—almost literally—sitting ducks.

And there was something more, something that had been nagging at the back of my mind since we had left Sde Boker and that was how they had found us in the first place. And how the chopper had zeroed in on us at Tlalim.

By the time we had passed Sderot and started slowing for our approach through the suburbs of Ashkelon, I was no clearer in my mind on either of those points.

We took a couple of detours and approached past the Ashkelon National Park and along the David Ben Gurion Boulevard. We came to a big circus with a fountain, crossed it, and suddenly we were on the beach. Another mile, maybe less, and we arrived at the marina. There was a plethora of bars and restaurants and a large mall, and you could imagine that at another time it would have been teeming with people. But right then, with the jets screaming overhead every fifteen minutes or so and the choppers prowling the northern border of Gaza just seven miles down the coast, the place was quiet, and most of the bars and restaurants were closed.

Gallin pulled over and parked by the steps down to the marina. We climbed out and moved quickly down the stairs. Broad, illuminated signs offered us Guinness and waffles and flooded the stairs with amber light. We ignored their empty promises and crossed the broad walkway toward a large, white iron gate that gave access to the piers where the boats were moored. Beside the gate, there was a hut. The window in the hut was glowing softly, and when we arrived and peered inside, we found a security guard watching a small TV.

The general smiled at him. "Good evening, Josh. How's life?"

"Hey, General Drake! Good to see you! Been a long time."

The general laughed. "Too often life gets in the way of pleasure. Listen, Mr. Rappaport wanted me to show his friends the yacht. Can you let us in?"

"Sure thing."

He reached for his mouse, but the general gave another laugh. "There is just one other thing." He reached in his pocket and pulled out his wallet. From there he extracted a hundred bucks and handed them over. "I came out in such a hurry I left the keys at the hotel. Have you got a spare set?"

Josh the security guard looked distressed. "Of course, General," he said, "but I would have to check with Mr. Rappaport or I could be in serious trouble. You don't mind if I call him?"

The general smiled. "Of course not. It's the least I'd expect."

He reached for his cell. I stepped in and smacked him on the jaw. He sagged back in his chair, I frisked him for his keys, found a huge bunch, and tossed them to the general. Meanwhile Gallin had squeezed in and was playing with the computer. The gate started to roll back. I stepped out, and Gallin took his cell, his mouse, and his keyboard.

We moved quickly down the pier, with the general sorting through the keys and Gallin looking over her shoulder and occasionally walking backward, watching the gate. I said to the general, "You know where it's moored?"

"Yes, he has his private mooring down at the end, on the right. It's the Lady Miriam, at the end there." He held up the keys with a green plastic tag poking up. "It's these."

I heard the gate clang closed, looked back, and saw Gallin tossing the cell, the mouse, and the keyboard into the harbor.

"That will delay proceeding for a bit at least." She pulled her cell from her pocket, dialed one digit, and put it to her ear. After a moment, she spoke fast, rattling in Hebrew. When she was done, she put the phone away and said, "We have a one-hour window. We need to move!"

We moved at a jog down the wooden pier and soon saw the private mooring ahead. But as we approached, I saw Gallin stop, and at the same time I saw three men standing at the stern of the large, white yacht. They were maybe forty yards away. One of them stayed where he was. The other two fanned out across the pier. The hairs at the back of my neck prickled, and I saw three more men approaching behind us. They had obviously been hiding in one of the boats and emerged as we passed.

The guy directly ahead of me had a big barrel of a chest with small, thin legs. He had a jaw like a megalith and hair cut so short you could see his scalp.

He said, "Don't do anything stupid." The accent was definitely not Israeli, more like South Africa.

"That's good advice for everybody," I said. "What do you want?"

Gallin had turned and was watching the guys behind us. The South African said, "It's simple. This doesn't need to be complicated. Nobody needs to get hurt. The general comes with us, you go on your way."

I laughed. "Right, we hand over the general and you shoot us dead where we stand. I don't think so."

"What makes you think we couldn't do that right now?"

I stepped to my left, slipped my left forearm painfully around the general's neck and placed the muzzle of the Sig against his temple.

"You want him alive. We want him alive too. But there is just one thing I want more than the general alive, and that's me alive. Am I prepared to negotiate and hand him over? Yes. But I need my guarantees."

The South African glanced at the guy beside him, then looked back at me. "Guarantees like what?"

"You let us get on the boat. You get the general, we get to sail away."

The general swallowed hard. "Take it easy, son."

Behind me, I heard Gallin's voice. It was cold and dangerous. It said, "Keep your hands where I can see them, boys. You'll probably kill me, but I'll take at least two of you with me. You want to play that game?"

A slow count of three told me they were unsure of their next move.

"Your move," I told the South African. "What's it going to be?"

TWENTY-ONE

He didn't answer, and I began to inch toward the gangway that led to the stern deck of the Horizon E18. The guy who had stayed by the boat watched me with obstinate eyes and didn't move. I knew he was trying to provoke some action on my part that would give them an opening to kill us and take the general. I held his eye for a long count to three and spoke quietly.

"Here's where you have to make a choice, pal. He dies, you die, or you both die. You pick, A, B, C, or all of the above."

He took a couple of reluctant steps away. I growled at Gallin, "Take the keys, go aboard. You know how to work this thing?"

She gave me a look that asked if I had any more stupid questions. She took the keys from the general and ran up the ramp. The South African said, "OK, that's enough. You have your boat. Now hand over the general."

I smiled. "I count six of you guys. I let the general go and I figure I'll be about three ounces of lead heavier."

They were getting restless, and I knew they were gearing up to rush me. The only thing holding them back was that they really badly wanted the general alive. They were standing in a semicircle around me with the guy who'd moved away from the stern just seven feet away. I could see him eyeing my hand. The South African said, "Come on, guy, it's over. There's nothing you can do. Just hand him over."

As he said it, the guy from the stern took a step toward me. Sometimes in life you just have to be brave and do crazy things, right? So real fast and real smooth, I reached out and plugged a slug right through his head. Before they registered what I had done, as his knees wobbled and he began to drop, I snapped my hand back and shoved the muzzle of the Sig under the general's jaw.

I grinned at the South African. "I don't think you believed I was serious. So I should explain. I am a mean son of a bitch and so is my partner. Now I know I am outnumbered, and I know you will probably kill me tonight whatever I do, but if I go down, I am going to hurt you as badly as I can. And you, you South African son of a bitch, will be the first to go down, even before the general. So let go of the idea that you hold all the cards, and let's see if we can reach some kind of an accommodation."

The South African had his hands up and was looking alarmed. He said, "OK, take it easy. I said nobody needs to die. You tell me. How do you want to do this?"

"Any minute now, this boat is going to start rumbling when my partner starts the engines. When that happens, two of your boys are going to release the moorings, and I am going to back up the gangway. At the top, I let the general go. He descends the gangway. You try anything, I shoot him in the back. We pull out; you go on your way."

"What's to stop you taking him on board with you?"

"Five guys with guns. The minute he crosses onto the deck, you'll blow us both away. You want him alive, but if he's in somebody else's hands, you'd rather have him dead. I know the score."

I had no idea if that was true or not, but as long as they believed that I believed it, I had a chance.

A moment later, the engines rumbled into life, and I began to back toward the gangplank, watching each one of them like a hawk. The South African pulled a weapon from behind his back and took aim at my head. His four remaining companions followed suit. I moved in tighter behind the general. An ace marksman could have made the shot, but we were moving, and the smallest deviation at fifteen or twenty feet could easily translate to the one or two inches needed to put the general's brains all over my shirt.

I said, "Do it right, boys, and you get your man and you get to go home. Stay cool." I was practically at the top of the ramp and praying fervently that Gallin was watching and listening. I paused with my heel on the gunwale, and I could see the boys getting real antsy. Mr. South Africa strode up to the gangplank, waved his pistol at me, and shouted, "OK! That's enough! Send him down!"

"OK," I said. "I'm going to let him go. But you lower your weapons till I am on the boat and he is on the pier." They hesitated. I put the gun to the general's temple and bellowed, "*Do it now!*"

As I yelled the words, I jumped backwards, dragging the general with me. Gallin had gotten the message, the engines surged, the prow rose up high, and we plowed away from the pier, leaving a chaos of foam and breakers behind us. Shots rang out, but we were well away, lying flat on the deck as we plowed toward the lighthouse and the open Mediterranean.

I sat up and looked at the general. He was up on one elbow, watching me and trying to steady his breathing.

"You had me scared, Mason. You had me worried there for a moment."

I got to my feet and held out my hand. "I'm a man of my word, General. I hope you are."

He took my hand, I pulled him up and we went inside the cabin. Gallin said, "You need to find some charts. I'm going north and a little west, which should get us to Cyprus, but a chart and a plotted course would help."

"I'll get them." It was the general. "I know where they are."

He made his way to a drawer, and I returned to the stern to look at the lights of Ashkalon Marina as it fell behind us. To the right, I could still see the choppers flying over Gaza, and to the left the flashes, like sheet lightning flickering and glowing across the northern border in Lebanon.

Behind me, I could hear the general talking to Gallin, discussing the correct bearing to arrive at Limassol, in Cyprus. I heard him say it was a hundred and ninety nautical miles, and as I thought absently that Gallin could do it in an hour if we were driving in her car, I saw a glimmer of light, like a flashlight on the sea, maybe a mile behind us. Then there was another, and a third.

I stepped back inside and said, "We have company. Does your friend keep any weapons on board?"

He nodded. "Of course. This close to Gaza, smart people tend to be armed. What is it?"

"Hard to tell at this distance, but it looks like a couple of fast launches, maybe three."

He gave another nod. "There are a couple of rifles in the cabin."

He went forward to get them, and Gallin gave me a look. "How'd they know?"

"I've been asking myself that since the Zen temple."

"It doesn't make sense."

The general emerged from the cab carrying two HK416s and some spare magazines. I took one, and we went out to the stern. We lay on our bellies and crawled to the gunwale. We were moving fast and skipping over the small waves. I could see clearly now that we had four pursuers. They were maybe half a mile away and closing fast. They were small, two-man launches skipping over the small waves and raising great sheets of spray high above the surface. Aiming was going to be difficult.

"We concentrate our fire," I told the general. "We both take the nearest target and alternate bursts. Take him and go for the next."

He nodded. "Agreed."

As they approached to within a hundred yards, they began to fan out, two directly behind us and one on either side. Now I could see there were two in each boat, one driving and the other carrying a rifle. There was no right choice. They were much faster and more agile than we were and could easily outrun us. Plus, to be sure of a kill, skimming over the water at that speed and with so much movement, we had to concentrate our fire on one target at a time. But that meant while we were shooting at one, the other three were closing in for the kill.

I knew Gallin was on my left, our pursuers' right, so that made up my mind for me. The guys who were beginning to draw level on my left had to go. I touched the general's arm and nodded at the launch. We both took aim and opened up. The sea exploded around them, and the windshield shattered. The HK416 puts out 850 rounds a minute. Between us, our rate of fire was one thousand seven hundred rounds a minute, or twenty-eight rounds a second. After three seconds, we had put eighty-four rounds in their direction. The boat veered wildly, stood vertical, and capsized.

But those three seconds were all they needed for two of the launches to surge up on our right flank while the third raced in behind us, showering the back of the boat with lead. Almost simultaneously, the two launches on our right started strafing the side of the yacht. Gallin veered away from them, sending me and the general sliding across the deck.

Somehow I managed to scramble to the gunwale again as she straightened up, and I put three rounds into the windshield of the launch behind us. The general scrambled on his belly to the far side, put his rifle over the side, and fired blindly. A second later, the side of the deck exploded in a shower of fiberglass as a hail of molten lead tore into it.

At that moment, an absolute certainty dawned on me that this was how it all ended. A fraction of a second later, the hail stopped. Their magazines had dried up. I called to the general, "*You alive?*"

As I did so, I got on one knee and emptied my magazine into the boat behind us. I saw the driver's head explode and a stream of gore spray out behind him. I noted his rifleman was already dead from my earlier salvo. I dropped the magazine and rammed another one in. I heard the furious rattle of automatic fire. Gallin weaved and swerved again, then started to describe a wide circle to her right, giving us a clear shot at the two launches' right flanks.

We took up positions on the port side and opened fire. But they had pulled back and were simply pacing us. I noticed then that we were slowing, and there was a powerful stench of fuel on the water.

I heard Gallin's voice then, coming from inside.

"*We're hit! We're losing fuel! Will somebody please kill those bastards!*"

I glanced behind us. The launch was idling, maybe twenty feet away. I leaned into the cabin and shouted to Gallin, "Kill the engines. You listen to me and listen good! I am going over the side. I need one minute. During that time you take pot shots at them. In one minute, you hail them and tell them you surrender. Your engines are dead. They can come and get the general."

He stared at me. "You're abandoning me?"

"I told you I am a man of my word, General. Like Schwarzenegger, I'll be back."

I slipped over the side and swam silently under the water as far as the launch. There I reached up and gripped the side, hauled myself in, and slid onto the rear bench. As I did so, I heard the stutter of automatic fire.

The windshield of the launch was gone, and there was shattered glass all over the two dead guys in the front. I took their weapons and stashed them in back, then, with great difficulty, I dragged them over the side and let them slip into the water. After that, I eased up nice and slow to the starboard side of Rappaport's dead vessel. I secured the front mooring rope to the stern deck and slipped back onto the yacht. To Gallin, I said, "OK, now."

She used the boat's loudhailer, telling them we were done, adding that we were taking a dinghy, we were leaving the general aboard, and they could come and get him. The reply came almost immediately.

"*Throw your weapons overboard.*"

While the general and Gallin complied, I grabbed two bottles of whiskey and two of gin from the drinks cabinet, saturated several cloths I found in the galley, and stuffed them in a plastic bowl. Then I filled the bowl up with the remainder of the spirits. I snapped at the general, "Give me your matches!"

He stared at me a second, said, "Jesus...!" and handed them over. "*Get in the launch!*" I yelled. "*Now!*"

Outside, I could see the other two launches approaching. The gunmen were on their feet with their rifles at their shoulders. I stepped out onto the deck, lit a match, and dropped it in the bowl. The beautiful, translucent blue flames leapt high, generating the intense heat spirit flames do. The kind of heat you need to ignite fuel oil. I hurled the plastic tub over the side and leapt across the deck to dive over onto the launch. Gallin was already at the wheel. The air shook, and a wave of heat washed over us as the yacht's leaking fuel ignited. The screams of the four men caught in the inferno were soon drowned out by the roar of the launch's engines.

We hurtled into the blackness ahead, and I managed to claw my way into a sitting position. For a moment, I was hypnotized by the flickering amber glow on the small waves and the back of Gallin's and the general's heads.

"What's the range on these things?" I asked eventually.

Gallin gave a small shrug. "Maybe four hundred nautical miles. We have plenty to get us there in three or four hours, if we don't get lost."

"Has this thing got GPS?"

She looked over her shoulder at me and smiled. "Not that kind of boat, Mason."

"But you have a compass in your head because you've been sailing since you were a kid, right?"

"Yup."

"Right. General, I need your shoes and your watch."

He turned and frowned at me. "What?"

I made the face of weariness and said, "You heard me."

He pulled off his Rolex and his handmade Italian shoes. I took them in my hands and threw them overboard into the sea.

"What the hell?"

I pointed at him. "Everywhere you go, they follow. Somebody bugged you. Now I am assuming it's not in your shirt or in your pants, and they didn't shove it up where the sun don't shine. So that leaves your shoes and your watch. If you are a religious man, general, pray there is nobody waiting for us at Limassol."

With that, I gave in to the demands of my exhausted body and fell into deep, black oblivion.

TWENTY-TWO

NERO WAS SITTING BESIDE A LARGE TURQUOISE swimming pool with a vast, Mediterranean sky behind him. We were on a cliff on Malta. Apparently he believed that when in the Mediterranean, he should wear bizarre clothes. He now had on beige slacks, a white shirt open to his solar plexus, and very black sunglasses.

"It was," I told him, "impossible to carry out the mission without finding out first what was on the drive."

He raised a pudgy finger. "Alex, do I need to remind you that you did not, in fact, carry out your mission? In fact, you personally destroyed the very item you were tasked with recovering." He showed me a palm to stop me protesting. "However, it would be churlish to hold that against you in the circumstances. Captain Gallin has informed me that your conduct, and your aim, were both beyond reproach."

"That's real big of you, sir. I have some questions."

"I rather feared you might."

"Does this Cabal really exist? Surely this is fantasy, science fiction..."

"Utterly. It is the product of Geller's and Orlev's fevered imaginations. What we did not know at the time was that they had both been using ayahuasca, an Amazonian psychoactive drug, for a couple of years to expand their consciousness, and it had driven them into deep paranoia."

I stared at him in stunned silence for a good five seconds. It had not been the response I was expecting. I looked at Gallin and saw she was frozen with her beer halfway to her mouth. I said, "But General Drake, the evidence we brought..."

"General Drake flew to Washington DC earlier this morning, where he will be thoroughly debriefed by ODIN interrogators. An initial review of his evidence suggests much of it is fabricated—"

"We saw it!" I blurted out. "It was real!"

"No doubt it seemed that way. You were both fatigued, and you were seriously weakened by your recent injury. You may even have been feverish. However, he will be debriefed and, if necessary, he and his wife will be relocated with new identities."

"But if the evidence he gave us was the evidence he had given Geller and Orlev, and that had made the flash drive so vitally important that people were gunning for us from DC to London, Menorca and Israel..."

"Are you asking me to tell you what was on the flash drive, Alex?"

"Yes."

"No. Have you any other questions?"

Gallin said, "Yes! I have. Are the United States, the United Kingdom, and Europe sliding toward a dystopian totalitarian regime, driven by a cabal of super privileged despots who have their meetings at Bilderberg summits and the World Economic Forum?"

"That is at least three, possibly four questions, Captain. The answer comes in two parts. I have to say"—here he paused and looked deep into her eyes, and then mine—"I have to say that that is an absurd question, and of course it is fantastic nonsense. I would also add, Captain, Alex, use your own intelligence. Look around you. What do you see?"

I felt a hot coal of anxiety burn in my gut. I lowered my voice and spoke rapidly. "But if there is any truth at all in what the general told us, we have to act!"

"Alex!" I stopped. He regarded me a moment from under hooded eyes. "Unless you wish to become a marginalized crank, laughed at in the media, regarded as insane, you will keep your views on this subject strictly private. You both performed your duties with admirable intelligence and foresight, and your dedication, well beyond the call of duty, will be suitably rewarded." He levered himself to his feet. "I strongly recommend a good two-week vacation at some luxury resort for the two of you, where you can digest everything that has happened and process it, as they say these days. The Company will pay, naturally."

We watched him move across the terrace of the villa toward the sliding glass doors. There he stopped and turned. "I was at Woodstock, you know. I was just sixteen, and very skinny. *The Lord of the Rings* was our Bible back then, freedom was the great dream, the freedom of the individual. And we all dreamed of what it would be like when the Age of Aquarius dawned. Harmony and understanding, sympathy and trust abounding, no more falsehoods or derisions, and the mind's true liberation..." He trailed off, then added, "Who could have dreamed it would be like this? Take nothing at face value, assume nothing, and be very, very careful who you trust."

He left, and we sat staring at each other until Gallin said, "What the hell was that?"

After a moment, I said, "A lie. We were never read in, and we still aren't."

"That's not good enough."

"Talk to your dad. I'll tell you one thing. Nero picked us for the job because he knew we would disobey him and dig deeper than we were supposed to."

"How can you know that?"

"I know him, and he as much as told us to keep digging. He told us to take the vacation and discuss what had happened and to keep it to ourselves. He as much as instructed us to keep digging."

She frowned. "You reckon?" Then she grinned. "We could use a holiday."

"Yeah," I said. "I sure could. We could discuss that ranch in Wyoming..."

We spent the afternoon relaxing and in the evening went to the local bar for a supper of beer and tapas. It was while I was sipping my beer and looking at the menu that she leaned forward and touched my arm. I followed her gaze to the television on the wall just inside the bar and saw a scene of chaos on what should have been a pretty, leafy street. There were three ambulances and at least half a dozen patrol cars. There were crowds and police tape and cops telling people to move back. Amid the chaos there was the smoking wreck of what had once been a luxury sedan, perhaps a Mercedes.

We both stood and went to lean on the doorjamb. English is one of the two official languages in Malta, and the BBC news was being broadcast in English. There was a guy with a microphone talking into the camera.

"...so far there are very few details available. What we do know is that Mr. Harrison, the former governor of the state, was driving along Carson Street having had lunch at Glen Eagles with a couple of his associates. It is not clear yet whether those associates were with him in the car. It appears he was headed to Carson City's State Capitol for a meeting with the governor when his car simply exploded."

The anchor's voice cut the guy short and asked, "Do we know, David, who the associates were...?"

David pressed his ear and said, "Chris, I am just hearing that his associates, who were in fact in the car with him, were William Portos of the Portal Operating System giant and Mitch Hansen, the CEO of the Skyhawk Defense Technology Corporation. It seems all three were killed instantly. That is three of the United States' preeminent industrialists killed instantly in a matter of seconds. The Carson City Police Department are not saying as yet whether they are treating this as a bizarre accident or as a terrorist attack..."

Gallin turned to me and stared into my face. "Son of a bitch."

I thought about it. "A warning shot across the bows?"

We returned to our table and sat in silence for a moment.

"We are at war," I said.

She nodded. "A nation can survive its fools. It can even survive the ambitious, but it cannot survive treason from within. The enemy at the gates is less formidable, for he is known, and carries his banner openly. But the traitor moves freely among those within the gates, his sly whisper rustling through all the alleys, heard in the very halls of government itself. We are at war, Mason, but who with?"

We were silent for a long time, staring unseeing at our menus. Finally I sighed and said, "This is something we need to discuss very carefully and very privately."

She looked up from her menu and said, "I agree, Mason. I say Goa. Goa at this time of year is..."

She hunched her shoulders, and I put in, "Conducive to contemplative thought and meditation?"

"Yeah," she said. "That. You feel like ordering some champagne and celebrating?"

"I do. Life is short." And I called the waiter.

DON'T MISS ANYTHING!

If you want to stay up to date on all new releases in this series, with these authors, or with any of our new deals, you can do so by joining our newsletters below.

In addition, you will immediately gain access to our entire *Right House VIP Library,* which currently includes *ORIGINS*—a full length prequel novel to *ODIN.*

righthouse.com/email

(Easy to unsubscribe. No spam. Ever.)

ALSO BY DAVID ARCHER

Up to date books can be found at:
www.righthouse.com/david-archer

ROGUE THRILLERS
Gates of Hell (Book 1)
Hell's Fury (Book 2)
Ice Burn (Book 3)

JACOB HUNTER THRILLERS
The Kyiv File (Book 1)
The Bogota File (Book 2)
The Havana File (Book 3)
The Amsterdam File (Book 4)

PETER BLACK THRILLERS
Burden of the Assassin (Book 1)
The Man Without A Face (Book 2)
Unpunished Deeds (Book 3)
Hunter Killer (Book 4)
Silent Shadows (Book 5)
The Last Run (Book 6)
Dark Corners (Book 7)
Ghost Operative (Book 8)
A Fire Burning (Book 9)
Dawnlight (Book 10)

ALEX MASON THRILLERS

Odin (Book 1)
Ice Cold Spy (Book 2)
Mason's Law (Book 3)
Assets and Liabilities (Book 4)
Russian Roulette (Book 5)
Executive Order (Book 6)
Dead Man Talking (Book 7)
All The King's Men (Book 8)
Flashpoint (Book 9)
Brotherhood of the Goat (Book 10)
Dead Hot (Book 11)
Blood on Megiddo (Book 12)
Son of Hell (Book 13)
Merchant of Death (Book 14)

NOAH WOLF THRILLERS
Code Name Camelot (Book 1)
Lone Wolf (Book 2)
In Sheep's Clothing (Book 3)
Hit for Hire (Book 4)
The Wolf's Bite (Book 5)
Black Sheep (Book 6)
Balance of Power (Book 7)
Time to Hunt (Book 8)
Red Square (Book 9)
Highest Order (Book 10)
Edge of Anarchy (Book 11)
Unknown Evil (Book 12)
Black Harvest (Book 13)
World Order (Book 14)
Caged Animal (Book 15)

Deep Allegiance (Book 16)
Pack Leader (Book 17)
High Treason (Book 18)
A Wolf Among Men (Book 19)
Rogue Intelligence (Book 20)
Alpha (Book 21)
Rogue Wolf (Book 22)
Shadows of Allegiance (Book 23)
In the Grip of Darkness (Book 24)
Wolves in the Dark (Book 25)

SAM PRICHARD MYSTERIES
The Grave Man (Book 1)
Death Sung Softly (Book 2)
Love and War (Book 3)
Framed (Book 4)
The Kill List (Book 5)
Drifter: Part One (Book 6)
Drifter: Part Two (Book 7)
Drifter: Part Three (Book 8)
The Last Song (Book 9)
Ghost (Book 10)
Hidden Agenda (Book 11)

SAM AND INDIE MYSTERIES
Aces and Eights (Book 1)
Fact or Fiction (Book 2)
Close to Home (Book 3)
Brave New World (Book 4)
Innocent Conspiracy (Book 5)
Unfinished Business (Book 6)

Live Bait (Book 7)
Alter Ego (Book 8)
More Than It Seems (Book 9)
Moving On (Book 10)
Worst Nightmare (Book 11)
Chasing Ghosts (Book 12)
Serial Superstition (Book 13)

CHANCE REDDICK THRILLERS
Innocent Injustice (Book 1)
Angel of Justice (Book 2)
High Stakes Hunting (Book 3)
Personal Asset (Book 4)

CASSIE MCGRAW MYSTERIES
What Lies Beneath (Book 1)
Can't Fight Fate (Book 2)
One Last Game (Book 3)
Never Really Gone (Book 4)

ALSO BY BLAKE BANNER

Up to date books can be found at:
www.righthouse.com/blake-banner

ROGUE THRILLERS
Gates of Hell (Book 1)
Hell's Fury (Book 2)
Ice Burn (Book 3)

ALEX MASON THRILLERS
Odin (Book 1)
Ice Cold Spy (Book 2)
Mason's Law (Book 3)
Assets and Liabilities (Book 4)
Russian Roulette (Book 5)
Executive Order (Book 6)
Dead Man Talking (Book 7)
All The King's Men (Book 8)
Flashpoint (Book 9)
Brotherhood of the Goat (Book 10)
Dead Hot (Book 11)
Blood on Megiddo (Book 12)
Son of Hell (Book 13)
Merchant of Death (Book 14)

HARRY BAUER THRILLER SERIES
Dead of Night (Book 1)
Dying Breath (Book 2)

The Einstaat Brief (Book 3)
Quantum Kill (Book 4)
Immortal Hate (Book 5)
The Silent Blade (Book 6)
LA: Wild Justice (Book 7)
Breath of Hell (Book 8)
Invisible Evil (Book 9)
The Shadow of Ukupacha (Book 10)
Sweet Razor Cut (Book 11)
Blood of the Innocent (Book 12)
Blood on Balthazar (Book 13)
Simple Kill (Book 14)
Riding The Devil (Book 15)
The Unavenged (Book 16)
The Devil's Vengeance (Book 17)
Bloody Retribution (Book 18)
Rogue Kill (Book 19)
Blood for Blood (Book 20)
The Cell (Book 21)
Time to Die (Book 22)

DEAD COLD MYSTERY SERIES
An Ace and a Pair (Book 1)
Two Bare Arms (Book 2)
Garden of the Damned (Book 3)
Let Us Prey (Book 4)
The Sins of the Father (Book 5)
Strange and Sinister Path (Book 6)
The Heart to Kill (Book 7)
Unnatural Murder (Book 8)
Fire from Heaven (Book 9)

To Kill Upon A Kiss (Book 10)
Murder Most Scottish (Book 11)
The Butcher of Whitechapel (Book 12)
Little Dead Riding Hood (Book 13)
Trick or Treat (Book 14)
Blood Into Wine (Book 15)
Jack In The Box (Book 16)
The Fall Moon (Book 17)
Blood In Babylon (Book 18)
Death In Dexter (Book 19)
Mustang Sally (Book 20)
A Christmas Killing (Book 21)
Mommy's Little Killer (Book 22)
Bleed Out (Book 23)
Dead and Buried (Book 24)
In Hot Blood (Book 25)
Fallen Angels (Book 26)
Knife Edge (Book 27)
Along Came A Spider (Book 28)
Cold Blood (Book 29)
Curtain Call (Book 30)

THE OMEGA SERIES
Dawn of the Hunter (Book 1)
Double Edged Blade (Book 2)
The Storm (Book 3)
The Hand of War (Book 4)
A Harvest of Blood (Book 5)
To Rule in Hell (Book 6)
Kill: One (Book 7)
Powder Burn (Book 8)

ABOUT US

Right House is an independent publisher created by authors for readers. We specialize in Action, Thriller, Mystery, and Crime novels.

If you enjoyed this novel, then there is a good chance you will like what else we have to offer! Please stay up to date by using any of the links below.

Join our mailing lists to stay up to date -->
righthouse.com/email
Visit our website --> righthouse.com
Contact us --> contact@righthouse.com

facebook.com/righthousebooks
x.com/righthousebooks
instagram.com/righthousebooks